Wherever You Are, You Are On The Journey

Conversations in a Coffee Shop
Book 1

Susan Jones

Contents

Personal Introduction
— Welcome!

It's easy to fear you've fallen off the religious journey. It's easy to assume you aren't spiritual as you don't fit into organised religion. It's easy to see the spiritual journey as no longer relevant. Others' ideas of the journey can mess with our heads.

I usually followed the 'right' moves in the Christian church I was raised in. Frequently I feared I'd left the 'right' path and was wandering lazy meadows like the truant Little Red Engine of my childhood story book. I often felt, like the Little Red Engine, that I'd disobeyed the injunction to, 'Stay on the rails no matter what!'

Other friends have long since given up on church. Even in my childhood there was little social need to be a church member anymore. Saying you went to church brought you more embarrassed, incredulous looks than respect or admiration. Church was no longer what everyone did on a Sunday. It didn't mean much to others. Saying I was a Presbyterian minister was a conversation stopper.

This cultural change was starkly illustrated six years ago on my first Maundy Thursday in a new inner-city parish. At 6.45pm I was at the front of the church setting up an intimate space with candles, stones, and a bowl for footwashing later. I'd sourced reflective music and planned lots of silence among carefully written words. As I'd nearly finished my preparations, a group gathered at the other end of the church. New to the parish, I was surprised how many there were and how young, expecting more grey heads.

Then a local member led half the group down the aisle and through an internal door to the church's conference centre behind. The young attendees were NOT coming to my mindfully meditative Maundy Thursday commemoration. No. They'd enrolled online (sight unseen) for a six-week mindfulness course beginning that evening in a hired conference room. Google maps had led them to the street address but had not distinguished church and centre.

What a symbol, I thought then and have done many times since, of what is going on for church, younger generations and the search for soul. They and we participated that evening in much the same meditative quality of activity in the same building but within very different contexts. The mindfulness group trusted an unknown secular instructor more than an established church and minister. For them, church history and 'baggage' obscures any deeply satisfying spirituality available within. It is not that they are not looking, but that they are looking in a different place.

Because I was around church and spiritually minded people, I kept being reminded that there is an inner spiritual journey to negotiate. I've found however, that it is wider and freer than I was taught. To my utter relief, I've learned I am always on that journey simply by virtue of being human. To be human, I discovered, is to be spiritual. Hence the title of this book. Wherever you are, you too are on the journey, (doing it your way, I hope.)

It is easy to lose sight of our inner convictions as we stumble, fall, pick ourselves up, and deal with critical fellow-travellers. It is not easy to seek new directions, through mists of disillusionment and disenchantment.

In my experience, as I need resources, they come into my life. I hope it will be the same for you. In this novel you have come across part of Hope's journey. Not all of it may suit you right now. Here, though, are ideas and metaphors which may help with the questions buzzing round your head. These conversations seek to support re-enchantment of your journey. To help you move into post-critical thinking. I hope the book helps you understand the reasons for the changes in your thinking, and in other people's. I hope too that you will learn how important it is that we do change.

Imagine you and I are sitting in a coffee shop with our favourite beverage in front of us. Here are, in novel form, significant encounters. They have their origins in different conversations I've had with a variety of seeking human beings who were wrestling with questions, doubts and scepticism.

I bring to the table, as virtual conversation partners, some authors who helped me understand what is going on for us when we begin this phase of faith and stumble our way through it. I'm personally indebted to their courage. They've put out into the world their innermost thoughts on journeying through this still poorly mapped landscape. There are a few metaphors of my own in here too, images that came to me as I strove to show clearly what was going on for other seekers.

• • •

Enjoy the realisation that you are not alone.

Others have trod this way before you.

Others tread this way with you.

As you walk honestly in your truth, others will be able to follow in your footsteps.

We are a band of contemporary pilgrims, sisters and brothers and others together making the most significant pilgrimage of our lives.

There is a journey.

You are on it.

With us.

Susan Jones

1 — Faith is a series of stages, not a destination

The growl of the coffee grinder and hiss of steam from the espresso machine fills the air. The smell of freshly brewed coffee tantalises my nostrils. *The Cup* is my favourite coffee shop, just across from the church. The young gen Xers, and Y's with whom I work call it my second office. Exploring new ideas fits this bustling urban atmosphere. They seem to work here better than in the holiness of the Gothic-revival inner-city church across the busy street.

I remember Guy, a young accountant whom I met for coffee one day. He told me he was getting more courageous at accepting and living out his gay identity. But he found as he did, that his religious satisfaction sank. We drew rough graphs of his life experience on paper napkins at the table. They crossed and twisted apart to show that, as he came out more and more, and felt more at home in his identity, his church connections soured. I knew this didn't have to be the case. I knew he could be clear about his identity at the same time as owning and enjoying his spirituality. The religion offered in his suburban church and others like it, however, is not compatible with his reality and authentic orientation. I remember he took with him the crumpled, coffee-cup ringed napkin on which I'd scribbled, illustrating our discussion. So had many of my coffee-and-conversation partners before and since.

Hope is my companion in trim flat whites this afternoon, her straight black hair shining in the sunlight slanting through the coffee shop window, deep blue eyes animated beneath her heavy fringe. She is straight, in her early thirties, and is considering applying for ordination as a minister of our denomination. She isn't entirely sure what this will involve her needing to believe. She's just told me that of late, she is not as certain as before of some beliefs she had as a child and adolescent. As a preacher's kid she lived under her father's at first evangelical, then later, very liberal preaching. What is the truth?

As I listened to her story, I thought of my own religious experience. When I was younger, I wouldn't have known what label to put on my home church. Later, I used the term evangelical. Then I came to see my local church was fundamentalist. Life and faith were presented as black and white. In our local congregation we were expected to know what side we were on. We certainly knew it was vital to stay on that 'right' side to be acceptable within that community.

Even as a teenager, I noticed huge effort expended on getting people to 'make a decision for Jesus Christ.' Then more effort to get them to follow up with baptism (believers, immersion) and church membership. Looking back it seems like a farm with different paddocks. Everyone was urged to jump the fence into the 'saved' paddock. After you'd made that effort, though, it seemed grazing in that paddock was enough for the rest of your life (if you were morally good all the time).

It wasn't that the New Zealand Baptist church didn't believe in adult education. It did. Our local church ran 'All Age Sunday School' (copied from the American Baptists). An hour before morning worship, everyone could be in classes organised for their age group. Classes, however, did not encourage the type of questioning that allows our faith to evolve. We just learned more about the faith we already had and how to keep on living moral lives, being 'good.'[1]

Our family had lively conversations after Sunday morning church at our dinner table. These taught me you don't necessarily have to agree with everything the minister says. As minister succeeded minister, I also learned different clergy present the Gospel in a variety of ways. Even as a teenager, I noticed the quality is variable!

I wonder whether, being a preacher's kid, Hope didn't have that liberty. In her home, the minister carved the Sunday roast each week. She wouldn't have observed a variety of ministers, from whom to learn about difference.

Hope finished her story of her journey through faith and church thus far. She sat absently stirring her flat white, looking at me expectantly. I wondered where to start.

"Your journey is like mine," I said, "with a few differences. It wasn't until I did academic theology as a ministry candidate, that I really started to question. There I discovered the 'facts' of faith I'd learned in Baptist all-age classes are actually only a few of many possible theories or approaches to belief. It isn't 'one-way fits all.'"

Now I stirred my coffee absently.

"When I learned those varying approaches, it wasn't easy. I had moments of panic. They've now faded, but then, they were frightening. I'd been carefully brought up to deride what we called backsliders." I grinned, "A good Baptist girl knew it was Not a Good Thing to be One of Those."

Hope grinned. "Yes, I remember that categorising of people. There were those who really thought they had got being a Christian just right and judged others as just 'playing' at church. A bit arrogant, really."

I drew a paper napkin towards me and fumbled for a pen in my handbag. Why could I never put the pen away in the same pocket.

"One panic attack I do remember involved the Bible. I was studying the Gospel of Mark in a university undergraduate paper taught at a distance. We were two hours' drive from the university. We connected by audio with microphones in those pre-Zoom days. For homework one day, we were asked to look at a particular chapter of the Gospel. The task was to see what sections it could be divided into. Then we were to speculate why the editor arranged the sections that way."

I looked at Hope. "Internally, I went into panic mode. 'Editor?' My Baptist soul protested! Was the lecturer suggesting someone had been 'messing about' with The Bible? I said nothing, too scared to let my panic show. I remember the strong feeling that if the Bible is a jigsaw, it was falling apart before my eyes. It was a horrible moment. But, I went home and did the homework like the goody-two-shoes that I was."

I drew three oblongs one after the other on the napkin. "I found the chapter did have three sections; three different stories told by Jesus to three different groups of people."

Hope nodded as she looked at the napkin where I wrote in the boxes, 'Pharisees,' 'man born blind' and 'disciples.'

"It was only then I realised what I'd unconsciously been assuming. I'd assumed the three stories in the chapter happened chronologically. I assumed it was almost like first, Jesus telling a story in the morning. Then he told one in the afternoon. Then, I also assumed, the chapter ended with what he said in the evening. I could see these three sections easily enough. I didn't get why these stories had been put together like this. And that's assuming I was going to admit the existence of an editor. For me, the jury was out still on that issue!"

I glanced at Hope. She was absorbed.

"I found the answer in the next teleconference. I was still keeping quiet about my sense of panic. We were told Mark's Gospel is made up of several story 'sandwiches.' The 'bread' stories which come first and last might be of cynics or sceptics or opponents of Jesus. The 'filling' of that sandwich is a story of someone who understood Jesus' message. Like this one here," I said, pointing at the boxes on the napkin.

I drew three more boxes in a row, writing in them this time 'Gentiles,' 'unbelieving disciples' and 'a group of women.'

"Or in another chapter, the 'bread' of the sandwich might be stories about people who 'got' what Jesus was saying and doing. They are sandwiched around a story of someone or a group who was faithless or unbelieving. We are invited to notice that the people who 'got' Jesus were those formerly outcast or ignored. Lepers, women, blind men, or Gentiles seemed to 'hear' what Jesus was teaching. Orthodox followers or clergy didn't seem to understand him as well."

"That makes sense," murmured Hope, almost under her breath.

"Sitting there, my panic subsided. I realised these stories being positioned like this taught me more. More than a simple chronological list would have done. This way, something was highlighted which I might otherwise have missed. I remember I felt that the two-dimensional jigsaw Bible was falling apart. With this new information it was as if the Bible was re-forming in three dimensions before my eyes. Now I had more than the content of the story and all its interactions. I had more than my speculation as to what Jesus or the Gospel writers were meaning by the story. Now, as well, there was the effect of the placing of the story. The stories are 'conversing' with each other, like the walls in a freshly painted room reflect light and colour from each other."

We smiled at each other. "So, the panic could subside?" Hope asked.

"Yes," I replied, "it did. Though, there were other moments. I knew at the back of my mind that when I accepted a new idea, it would affect other long-held ideas down the track. Those moments weren't easy. They were shocking and traumatic. Looking back, however, those critical moments are helpful corners I turned. Round seemingly blind corners we find new landscapes. It took me a while to trust that discovery."

"It helps to know other people have these moments, I thought I was the only one," said Hope.

I nodded, sipping my cooling flat white. "One thing which helped me was discovering an intellectually respectable theory about stages in faith during my ministry training. When I trained as a teacher, I learned about Piaget's[2] theory of human development which goes in stages, so I understood the idea of a 'stage theory.' That meant I got the idea behind James Fowler's[3] theory of faith development. At first, the academic terms for the stages didn't help, but at least I got the broad concept. It was a great relief to understand that my own personal spiritual life is a path which I can travel on, out of the narrow fundamentalist 'paddock' of my youth."

I reached for another napkin and started drawing a series of six boxes linked together in line. "Later writers have simplified the language and the stages. M. Scott Peck[4] writes about four stages, different from Fowler's six. Marcus Borg[5] and Thomas Moore[6] streamline it down to three though they use different names for the stages. They're probably the easiest to follow, but I now use Fowler's six stages."

I drew four columns alongside the six boxes, each with names at the top: Fowler, M Scott Peck, Borg and Moore.

Hope moved her head to look at the napkin, tracing the series of boxes with her finger. "Where do you think I am?" she asked.

"Let me describe them and you can work out for yourself where you think you are at for the moment," I replied. I pointed at the first row of boxes.

"We tend to begin our spiritual journey and our life journey in a fairy tale-fantastical kind of mode. The Easter Bunny, Santa Claus and some nursery fairy tales[7] fit into this mode of thinking. Borg describes us as 'uncritical' about what we are thinking and reading. Moore says that we live in an 'enchanted' world at this stage."

I pointed to the first three rows of the line of boxes, shading them in, grinning at Hope as I did so.

Behaviour if involved in organised religion	Stages of thinking/ 'faithing'	Fowler	M Scott Peck	Borg	Moore
Sunday school stage	Child learns stories of the faith	Intuitive/ Projective (early Childhood)	Chaotic/ anti-social	Pre-critical Thinking	Enchantment
Sunday school and youth group stages	Stories are understood literally	Mythical/ Literal Faith (mid to late childhood)	Chaotic/ anti-social	Pre-critical Thinking	Enchantment
May join a religious community and begin to serve	Some abstract thinking, complies with community's rules of faith	Synthetic/ Conventional (Adolescence)	Formal/ Institutional	Pre-critical Thinking/	Enchantment
Questions church and faith, may leave organised religion	Question orthodox rules, concepts of faith community as previously taught	Individuative/ Reflective (Late Adolescence to early Adulthood)	Sceptic/ Individual	Critical Thinking	Disenchantment
Maybe still in a religious community which accepts and encourages wrestling with questions, or in a para-church group or book club that discusses progressive or mythological spirituality.	Piecing together what will be retained, new ideas and letting rejected ideas go	Conjunctive faith (Middle adulthood)	Mystical/ Communal	Post Critical Thinking	Re-enchantment
		Universalising Faith (middle to late adulthood)		Post Critical Thinking	Re-enchantment

"You just have to see a little boy in a spider man costume at the supermarket, or his slightly bigger sister in a tutu and princess tiara, to know they are in an enchanted place in their heads, far removed from the reality of boring grocery shopping!"

Hope laughed, "I used to think I was Cinderella!"

"Exactly, you've got it," I said. "There comes a day or a moment or a year when we begin to find this enchanted paradise is not what it seemed before. It might take a pandemic for us to question the omnipotence of God, or a science lesson where the theory of evolution leaves no room for the Creator God you've been taught about."

"Whatever that first jolt is, Borg says that's the moment when we begin to think critically. Moore says that's when we become 'disenchanted' with the fantasy world which is so bright and sparkling when we're young."

I move my pen to the fourth line of boxes and write in 'disenchantment' and 'critical thinking' under the headings for Borg and Moore.

"This is a difficult time to navigate. Some call it a mid-life crisis. My panic attack over the jigsaw of the Bible was one of those moments. We eagerly learn new things in science. We travel the world, discovering other religions have similar ideas to Christianity. As we do that, we don't always notice we've lost our innocence. We just begin thinking differently about the world and God and ourselves."

"Then the shock comes. We realise how much of what we've previously valued doesn't fit with new understandings."

"This moment can come like a bombshell. A close friend might change her mind about her faith. Or a spiritual mentor might fail us. It can be devastating. If you are actively worshipping in a conventional or conservative congregation, having these thoughts can leave you feeling alone and an outcast."

Hope nods. My pen moves back to the Fowler column of boxes and to Fowler's name for his third stage, named 'conventional.'

"Many conventional churches are not interested in questioning. Particularly questions which go beyond a certain line. That line is drawn differently in different congregations."

"Alan Jamieson is a New Zealand sociologist and senior pastor. He discovered that often clergy do not want to accompany their parishioners on this questioning journey. They know it has the potential for their members to leave the church or, (worse still!), disrupt it. His *A Churchless Faith* has interviews with people who have left the church. He uses Fowler's stages as a framework to analyse what was going on for them. You'd probably find his book interesting. Some interviewees reported their minister just avoided them. Other ministers actively stated, 'you're on your own with that kind of thinking.'"

Hope shifted in her seat. "I know my dad is pretty dismissive now of people who still think the way he used to think. He gets a little reactionary about it. That's why I don't think I can ask him about this kind of stuff," she muttered.

"No. That's the stage he's at. People behave according to their reactions to the stage they are in. There should be no shaming about entering this period of questioning, whatever you call it. It might be Borg's 'critical thinking,' Moore's 'disenchantment,' Fowler's 'individuative/reflective' stage, Scott Peck's 'sceptic/individual.'" My pen jumps across the row of columns. "Different names, but the same stage. This stage is vital if we are to grow in our faith. We need it to develop a spirituality adequate for 21st century adult life."

"I find it helpful to think of it as an invitation to mature in thinking and so 'grow up.' Sometimes, people who cut free of the church at this stage act like adolescents. They revel in lying in bed on a Sunday morning instead of sitting in that hard pew. Or they might begin to do things previously forbidden by the churches they attended. It's rather like teenagers testing their parents, only in this case the 'parent' is the church."

"So, what can people do about these bombshell moments at this stage?" asked Hope. "I think I need another cup of coffee. Same again for you?"

"Please."

I watched her as she went to the counter. She seemed lighter somehow than the young woman who'd come to me, brow creased and face serious. I remember how it helped me to understand there is a process broader than my own life which is known and described. It helps to realise it isn't just my own badness, rebellion or even a mental breakdown.

Hope returned. "What can people do when they get disenchanted?" she asked again.

"There's more than one possibility. Two, I think are tragic," I replied.

"First, the questioner may stop asking questions. They might repress their doubts and developing thoughts so they can remain an acceptable member of a congregation. Or they might keep quiet to remain a compliant member of the clergy. They then tend to develop a stilted, 'fake' spirituality which is easily picked up by others. The questioner, of course, thinks they are hiding their struggle."

I shifted in my chair. "If they're clergy, their sermons become dry, boring and irrelevant. If the frustrated questioner is a lay person, they may become an irregular church attender. Or, funnily enough, they may become an ardent rule follower, insisting that the 'Right' thing is always done. They hope that will keep their own uncomfortable question at bay."

"The other tragic possibility, is that the person who becomes disenchanted, finds no support in their church and leaves. Alan Jamieson's *A Churchless Faith* follows people like that. You probably know people who have done that?"

Hope nods quietly, her face shadowed. "My brother. My English teacher at school. He was a PK too.[8] Is that the only thing that can happen?"

"There's one other response which people like your father have followed. They don't cut themselves off completely. They move sideways like your dad did. For him it was into academia. It does mean they are moving sideways on the faith stage road. I think of it as them kind of veering off into a siding," I said.

I draw a curve from stage four to the side of the boxes.

"The pity is that they don't get the chance to wrestle with the new ideas about faith and fresh interpretations of the Bible. That's what's needed to retain a spiritual perspective, and not just end up with a liberal, rational, logical approach. I get the feeling you don't find that satisfying either?"

Hope shook her head.

"The ideal is that both the church congregation and minister welcome such questions," I continued. "They should recognise them as desirable even if they are disconcerting. Hopefully, they will see asking these deeper questions as another, but vital, stage of faith. In my fantasy, ideal world, a congregation will have a minister who has allowed herself to go there. She's let herself roll with the scepticism and entertain the questions – to 'live them.' I think it was the German poet Rainier Maria Rilke who said that.[9]

It's only possible to lead people through a stage if you've already been there. You have to experience the dissonance and resonance it brings to a spiritual journey to help others through it."

Our coffees arrive and the server clears the debris from our first cups. After she leaves, Hope asks another question.

"If you can find such an ideal situation, how does the journey go from here?" Hope's finger moves to the next box on the napkin, and she reads slowly. "Re-enchantment? Post critical thinking? What do those labels mean in real life?"

"Let's pretend you are 'allowed' by others or 'allow' yourself to revel in asking questions and living into them. Slowly, some things will begin to reconnect. This is what Moore calls 're-enchantment' and what Borg calls 'post critical thinking.' Fowler uses the word 'conjunctive' – you know, like conjunctions join parts of sentences together? M. Scott Peck's label for this stage is complex: 'mystical-communal.' The more you read, the more that will make sense."

"What you find is that the questions don't always have definitive answers. To your surprise, you find it's often enough simply to have questioned a previously held position or idea. For me, the questioning and re-integration stages have inter-mingled for years. In them we learn how faith operates in the human soul. We learn about what faith really is. We learn a deeper wisdom about ourselves. Of course, we always knew that wisdom takes a while to develop. That's why it's mostly older people who are the wise ones."

"How does this fit with church?" asked Hope. "The conventional churches don't seem to like questions being asked. 'Liberal' churches aren't into such a free-floating kind of 'spiritual' approach. It's like 'spiritual' becomes a dirty word in liberal circles."

I nod. "There is a disconcerting mismatch at this in-between stage. If you're disenchanted, rituals, customs, God-language, and worship services lose some of their comfort and attraction. Let's say you're attending a conventional church firmly anchored in that conventionality. By asking critical questions, you disrupt the seamlessness of belief and ritual, and challenge theory and practice. Other people, even your good friends, may not like the direction you're taking. If you have liberal friends, they might be embarrassed you're still taking the spiritual journey seriously."

Hope nods slowly. I can tell she has already experienced these kinds of reactions.

"There is no map for this journey, Hope. The destination can't be found on Google Maps. SatNav can't give us directions. Each of us will arrive at a highly individual accommodation. We'll find our own balance between what we think and feel and what we do. It might be quite different to what other people think and do and feel."

"You can find, however, a cohort of other seekers. Sometimes just a phrase will tell you that the person right in front of you is questioning and seeking too. Exactly what they are questioning may be a different area of religion or ritual or devotion. You know however, they're going through the same sifting process. Sometimes you'll find fellow seekers in books. I can recommend a few writers – I've already mentioned Borg." I write 'Marcus Borg, *Convictions*'[10] on the napkin.

Hope looks at her watch. "Oh! I have to go!" She picks up the napkin. "Can I take this? And can I text you to meet another time? I need to do some thinking."

"Certainly. Go well."

I raise my hand in a wave as she darts out the door. I'm glad she feels that discussing the stages have been helpful. I sit and reflect as I sip my rapidly cooling cup of coffee.

I remember well the emotions I experienced when I was at the same stage as Hope. It was like riding a scary rollercoaster. I felt not just vague discomfort, but real anger once my questioning got thoroughly underway. Others I met on the journey felt they had been deceived, hoodwinked or even manipulated by clergy or other church leaders. It's never pleasant to feel you have been duped.

I mused further. I've come to see that most people act as best they can from where they are on the journey. For instance, a minister or pastor might permanently reside in the more black-and-white second of Fowler's faith stages. That will be the stage they preach from. I now see there is no conspiracy holding a congregation in a certain place. Leaders speak out of their own experience (or lack of it). Usually, they genuinely feel they are doing the right thing by their congregation. They are, as yet, unaware of another way to think about belief and faith and trust. Hope's dad was at the end of his career as a parish minister. He now preached from the liberal position he had found, outside the usual faith journey. His move into an academic pastoral theology position must have been a relief.

Ironically, some leaders I knew became even more dogmatic. As they felt questions knocking at their own door, they tried hard to keep such unwelcome visitors away. Many leaders don't understand that letting the questions in, will, after an uncomfortable period, be better than spending all their spiritual energy barring the door against them.

My thoughts moved on to my occasional meetings with a childhood Sunday School teacher, youth leader or minister in later life. I remember sometimes being surprised, or even deeply shocked, to find that since I last interacted with them, they had moved on in their spiritual journeys.

Often, I'd been holding a conventional position because of my admiration for that person, only to find they no longer held it themselves! It takes a big internal struggle to see others move from my childhood perceptions of them. For a while I wondered resentfully why they couldn't have done it sooner. (Of course, had they been in a different position when I was younger, I may not have been ready for their ideas at the time).

I thought of Hope on her way back to work. I hoped she'd accept the invitation to question and grow. I wanted to help her with that. I wondered if she quite realised how differently her mind-set worked compared with that of the biblical writers. They, two millennia ago and more, set down the Big Story we followed in church from a completely different mind-set. That might be a good thing to talk about over our next coffee.

2 — Don't look now, but you're surrounded

I pushed open the door of *The Cup*. The aroma of coffee and cinnamon and familiar sounds of coffee-grinding and milk being frothed, greeted me. I loved coffee shops!

I ordered my flat white, then grabbed a table at the back. Hope and I might stand a chance of hearing each other here. She'd texted for another talk. I was interested to see how she would kick it off. Conversations went better when the questioner led the way. (Even when I thought I knew what the next topic for the journey should be!)

Hope rushed in, mouthing, "Sorry!" across the shop. She gave her order at the counter. "Last minute request for a hard-to-find item," she said apologetically as she slid into the booth opposite me. Hope worked in an antiquarian bookshop. Some books were indeed hard-to-find in the over-stocked, three-storey store. I often lost myself for hours there.

"No problem," I said.

She settled herself and her gear. Rummaging in her bag, she brought out the napkin from last week's conversation.

"I get what you were saying about stages," she plunged straight in. "I remember when I confused Jesus with the Easter Bunny, and God with Santa Claus. They all seemed to be one giant, mysterious person."

Her finger moved to the second stage of faith which we'd been talking about the previous week.

"I remember being so priggish when I was a teenager. I constantly disagreed with friends travelling a greyer route. I much preferred my black and white ideas about the Bible and stuff."

Her finger moved further along the row of stages.

"I recognise this conventional stage. It was good for a while. Dad was in this stage when I was in primary school."

Her finger moved on.

"Then I started university and did Archaeology 101. I found I had more questions than the church had answers. I knew Dad was working through questions too. But I didn't find his solutions appealing. I've been kind of coasting in church since then. Not really taking it all on board. Bible stories seem more make-believe than true. I don't think most of them could possibly have been real historical events. I guess university taught me to look for evidence-based facts. I don't find many of those in the Bible. My friends think religion is superstitious mumbo jumbo, not for thinking people at all."

"Funny you should start talking that way today," I said, "I was thinking that concepts like 'truth' and 'facts' and words like 'belief' and 'faith' and 'trust' would be good to follow up. Especially after looking at the faith stages last week. Did you decide which stage you think you are at now?"

Hope considered the napkin. Her finger moved to the disenchantment box.

"I guess I am more here than I've been prepared to admit. I think I am disenchanted in relation to conventional church options and in relation to where Dad has arrived at," she said slowly.

"Because I worship here," she said, jabbing the conventional and enchantment boxes, "it isn't comfortable to admit I am really here." Her finger moved to Moore's 'disenchantment' and across to Borg's 'critical thinking.'

"I'm critical of what the conventional church is teaching. I've been trying out a few different ones. I'm looking for a place to feel at home. None of them seem to be talking the same language I learned in university. Not even using language the world uses in general. Conventional churches seem to want you to check in your brain at the door. Liberal churches only want your brain, not your heart as well."

"There are so many places where there are gaps. Often reason falls down the cracks. No one ever quite addresses those disconnects fully, either." She sounded exasperated now.

I nodded. It all sounded familiar. I remember that mix well; confusion and frustration merging into anger some days. I thought I could help her here.

"I found one important key when I read my first Marcus Borg book. I'd been too afraid to read Borg. I knew a lot of people who were questioning more than I was. They were reading and recommending

Borg. I thought if I read him too, I would 'lose my faith.' I didn't want to find myself whizzing down what I thought would be a slippery slide."

"Then a friend I trusted recommended Borg's *Putting Away Childish Things*. It's a novel. Borg admitted, though, that he used the novel format to get a few teaching points across. Novel-wise it is sometimes a bit awkward."

"*Childish Things* is about a New Testament teacher in a North American liberal arts college. You get to see what she teaches and 'listen in' on class discussions. There are students from a conservative bible study group in class. They face off with more liberal students who are 'fans' of the professor. You get all sides of the argument."

"Sounds interesting," said Hope, writing the name of the book on her napkin.

"Kate, the professor in the book, explains how thinking changed in the 18th century."

I grab a fresh napkin from the box on the table just as our coffees arrive. I draw a long line with 0 at one end and 2000 at the other. I divide the line into two, putting 1000 at the mid-point. Then I put a mark about three quarters of the way long the second half of the line and write c.1750.

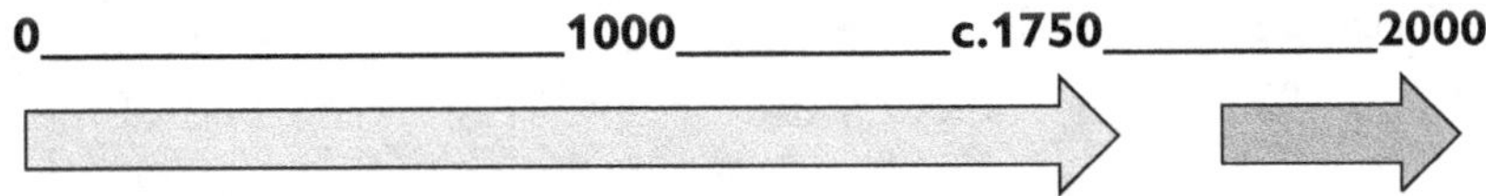

From 0 to 1750 I draw a long arrow and from 1750 to 2000 I draw another arrow. I shade it in, so it looks different from the first arrow.

"This is the major takeaway for me from the novel. Though it has other good stuff too. One disconnect which you're experiencing in church is because of the change in thinking that occurred in the Western world around 1750." I place my pen on the space between the two arrows. "There was one mode of thinking before that. There was quite a different one afterwards. In fact, the first kind of thinking goes way back before Jesus." I wave my pen to the left of the zero.

"This watershed around 1750 – not exactly in that one year but around that time – is called The Enlightenment. This was the period when a massive shift occurred from medieval to modern thought in Western civilization. As a result, science, and technology (as we know them today) started to rise at this time. You talked before about needing evidence-based facts. Gradually, during this period, reason, logic, and rationality came to be more important. They were considered more valuable than what we now call 'blind faith' or 'superstition' or 'belief,' (in the sense of believing something without any scientific proof)."

"Aha!" Hope mutters under her breath

"You're recognising this?" I ask.

"Yes, we have books at the shop about The Enlightenment."

"Right. Prior to The Enlightenment, (even during the Reformation, just a century or so before), the church was the main arbiter of what constituted truth." I marked in a short section on the timeline for the Reformation: 1517-1647.

"Both the Enlightenment and the Reformation are big movements that took decades, even centuries, to fully bed in. Each caused a massive mind shift. The Reformation marked the end of the domination of one way of doing Christianity. It created the beginnings of Protestantism, splitting off from Catholicism. In doing so, it implicitly endorsed the idea that the Mother Church didn't have to have the final say. It endorsed questioning the Church's rulings and theology."

"Kind of like a big society-wide stage four of faith," said Hope.

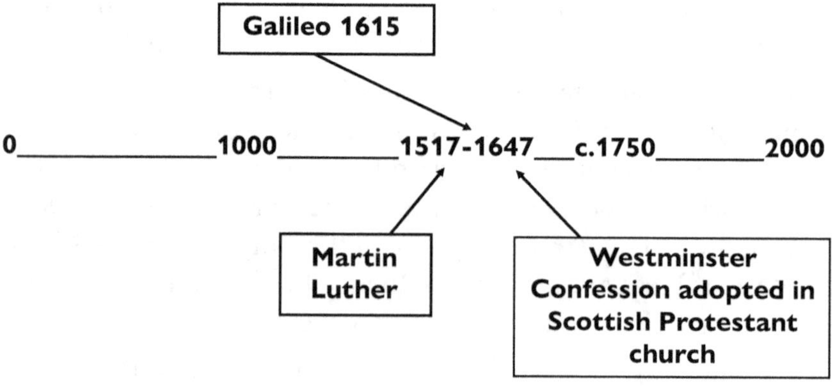

"Exactly! That's a great way of putting it," I replied.

"Science suffered under the church before The Enlightenment. Remember the Galileo argument about whether the earth or the sun was the centre of the universe? That came to a head in 1615."

I wrote 'Galileo 1615' with an arrow pointing to the middle of the reformation 'period' which I had drawn on the timeline.

Hope nodded. "I really must read more of the books in our shop," she said with a sheepish grin. "There's one about Galileo's daughter in the new section."

Circling my pen around the boxes around the timeline of the 16th and 17th centuries, I continued. "The Reformation and Enlightenment movements, and experimentation like Galileo's, were making reason, logic and empirical evidence more and more important. People were changing the values they used in deciding what was true or not. Reason came 'in,' and blind faith was on the way 'out.'"

"This became even more important in the 1800s, the 19th century. The University of Berlin, formed in 1848, could be called the first 'modern' university. That is, 'modern' as opposed to older universities which were medieval in origin. The first European universities (like Oxford, Bologna, Paris, and St Andrew's in Scotland) were formed by bishops gathering learned priests around them. Theology was known as the 'Queen of the Sciences.' It was the major subject in those universities when they were founded. Obviously, 'science' meant something different in that period from what it does today."

"The University of Berlin, however, intended to begin with a clean slate. At first, theology wasn't included in the curriculum because it was not thought rational enough. Eventually, through Friedrich Schleiermacher's work on the founding committee, the 'scientific discipline of Religion' was accepted as professional education for clergy. Theology was to function in the university just like law and medicine acted as professional education for lawyers and doctors. This began the divide between church faith and academic religion."[11]

Hope nodded thoughtfully. "I did a first-year paper in Theology. I thought it would help me with some of my questions. But it seemed like another language. It wasn't very closely related to what I heard in church. Does this explain that gap?"

I chuckled. "I'm glad you can relate to this. I'm getting carried away a little. The university-versus-church thing is a hobby horse of mine. The founding of Berlin illustrates the shift in thinking after The Enlightenment and on into the 19th century. Science and technology were ramping up at the same time. The industrial revolution in Britain is given the dates 1760 to 1840 in Wikipedia."[12]

I scrawled another box onto the napkin. "We're running out of room to add boxes to the timeline! It was a very busy period."

Pushing our empty cups aside, Hope pondered the mess of lines and boxes. "So, you were saying that people changed how they understood truth in the .... The Enlightenment?"

"Yes," I replied. "Slowly things became to be regarded as 'true' only if they had been observed. Or they were true if they were the result of an experiment. Anything 'true' had to be tested empirically. Arguments in science and in society were won by applying rationality and logic. It wasn't OK anymore to use belief without empirical evidence as an argument for truth."

"You can see the seeds of the present decline of Christianity here, can't you? The Bible was being taught literally in most churches. It was presented as a bunch of stories that happened, that were historically true. It didn't take long for the Bible to be discredited, especially for academics. They could not believe any longer that it was an empirically true and historically accurate document."

"These scientific methods started being used to study ancient manuscripts. This is called historical criticism. At the turn of the 19th and on into the 20th century, biblical scholars started to use these tools to study the Bible. That would have been too shocking earlier. It still shocks some stage two people today."

"Is that where your panic attack came from in that biblical course you did?" Hope asked. "The idea of an editor sounds like historical criticism to me. We did some of that in English Lit. when we were studying Chaucer."

"You're absolutely right. What an interesting degree you must have!"

"I guess it was," she replied. "Pity it wasn't more focused on a real-world job!"

"We need more coffee," I said. "My turn this week."

I got up and stretched my legs walking to the counter. Hope's degree subjects were helping her 'get' this complicated stuff. I thought of those who went into vocational training or trained on the job. No wonder they found it hard to suss out what was behind their dissatisfaction with church. Their feelings of dissonance were very real, but explanations were complex. Add too, the guilt we all felt daring to think differently from our priest, pastor, or minister. It seemed easier to squash questions down. Avoiding church altogether was a method many had used since The Enlightenment.

The shop had got busier since we'd arrived. I mused as I waited in line, that after all this historical background, there was still a key factor to cover. Why don't we realise how differently we think now? Why don't we understand that we don't think the same way as those who wrote the narratives in the Bible's First and Second Testaments? I shouldn't have worried. Hope gave me the link as soon as I sat down again.

"This idea of historical criticism doesn't seem shocking to me. I can see though, that it will have big ramifications for how to treat the biblical stories. You're saying the Bible isn't historically true, and we can't prove the events in it. Should we bother believing in it?" asked Hope.

"Another great question, Hope," I replied. She seemed to relax slightly. I realised that her questions hadn't been welcomed in the same way elsewhere.

"The thing is," I pointed to the two arrows and the gap between them, "we who live now have never thought in the way they thought before the Enlightenment." I tapped the first arrow. "We simply do not know their world." I moved my pen to the second arrow. "And… we don't realise, until someone points it out, that we now think in a post-Enlightenment way and have done since birth."

Below the timeline, I quickly drew a round bowl with a fish swimming in it. "We are like goldfish swimming round their bowl, surrounded by water. The goldfish doesn't know what water is. It hasn't had anything else to compare with it. It has always known water. It has always swum in water. It has never known anything else."

Hope's face lit up. "We're the same? We've always known post-Enlightenment thinking. We have always 'swum' in it. We've never known any other kind of thinking?"

"Exactly. Pre-Enlightenment thinking is another world. When we read unthinkingly anything written from a pre-Enlightenment mind-set, we read it from a post-Enlightenment perspective. Don't look now, but we are surrounded… by post-Enlightenment thinking. Consequently, ancient manuscripts don't seem 'true.' They don't quite make sense. They seem impossible, fantastical, or magical," I said.

Hope broke in, "…like fairy tales and fables and legends and…"

"… and, yes, the Bible. Pre-Enlightenment thinking was not concerned primarily with historical accuracy or objective truth. Yes, there were truths the community treasured. They were discussed and eventually written down, but in a symbolic fashion. That's why the nativity narrative has rich wise men from the East who travel a long way following a star. That's why there is an evil ruler, Herod, who means this unusual child harm. It's why a virgin birth is added to the story of Jesus' birth. All those events or characters are symbols giving us significant messages about Jesus, if we read the story from a pre-Enlightenment perspective. We frequently read it only from a post-Enlightenment point of view. Consequently, the story appears fantastical and historically impossible."

Hope looked startled by what I had just said. "So, the writers of some of the supernatural stories… weren't trying to pretend to those who read or listened to them being told, that they actually happened?" She thought for a moment. "What is the point then, of a story if it didn't actually happen?"

"Think for a minute, Hope and re-run that question you just asked. It's a very post-Enlightenment question, isn't it? You, like all of us living now, have been trained to take most notice of stories that are historically accurate. You react most favourably to stories which have been proven to be true in the sense of actually having happened."

Hope thought carefully. I could see her repeating the question she had asked to herself silently, then she grinned. "You're right!" She spread her arms dramatically, making jazz hands and waggling them to and fro. "I am a daughter of The Enlightenment!" she laughed.

I laughed too at the mischievous look on her face. We both then laughed at the surprise on the approaching waiter's face as he stopped short, and just avoided knocking our coffees onto the floor. We stopped talking while we got rid of empty cups and accepted the full ones. Then I took up the conversation again.

"The danger is in what people decide, in answer to the question 'What's the point?' They can conclude, because the Bible isn't full of historically accurate stories, that it is worthless. Then they may stop looking for meaning within the scriptures. But there is and always will be lots of meaning and significance to be found there."

"How do you get hold of that meaning and significance?" asked Hope. "I don't want to go back to being an uneducated medieval peasant in order to cope with church. But, I want more heart connection than I get in churches that emphasise education and intellect."

"Of course, you don't. You don't have to. We need to use our discoveries as post-Enlightenment people to let us see into the mind-set of Pre-Enlightenment writers. Then we can look for the symbols being used. We can find the metaphors with which scripture is stuffed. We can search for meanings encased deep within the obvious narrative. Underneath all the small stories is the Big Story which is the point. The Big Story was the point then and it is the point now as well. It is the story of how we can live a full and significant human life. It's a highly relevant Story, whether we live in the first or the 21st century."

"A biblical scholar, John Dominic Crossan, has been looking into this. He said this amazing thing, which pokes some fun at those who try to be great rational liberals. He said: (I just love this quote!)

> My point is not that those ancient people told literal stories
> and we are now smart enough to take them symbolically,
> but that they told them symbolically and we are now dumb
> enough to take them literally."

"Then, as if he hadn't made us squirm enough, he adds:

> They knew what they were doing: we don't."[13]

"He's saying we tend to throw out the stories because we think they are primitive, literal and gauche. If we do that, then we are throwing out rich symbols and metaphors. These are the symbols and metaphors which tell us much, much more than the simple storyline on the page."

"We don't have to become medieval peasants to believe in and use the Bible for our spiritual lives. But we, as 21st century, intelligent readers, must look at the Bible in a wholly different way. We need to do this knowingly. We will need all our post-Enlightenment knowledge to explore the symbolic depths of pre-Enlightenment manuscripts."

Hope was nodding. "Yeah, that makes sense… I think."

"David Tacey, an Australian scholar, put it this way (another quote I love!),

> …religion is not delusional but metaphorical. It is only delusional if we take the metaphors literally. Once we understand this, a lot of puzzling things make sense."[14]

I added, "There are some stories you can't accept at face value, as a Post-Enlightenment person. They can, however, still be useful in your life. Tacey warns against being too quick to abandon what seems strange and difficult. He says: 'The atheists throw out too much, and there is precious cargo in religion that "enlightened" people are losing.'[15] I like that phrase 'precious cargo.'"

Hope grinned broadly. "I don't get all that's involved – I'm sure there is a lot more. And I'm interested in finding out about the puzzling passages. But I feel less of an idiot already. I felt stupid wanting to still be a spiritual person. Most of my friends think church and the Bible are a joke. Talking with you, being spiritual and being Christian turns into a 'grown-up' activity. Can you email me those two quotes with their references? I must see if I can get those books."

"Sure. We need to talk a lot about what Tacey has to say on the subject. He's the best author I've read in this area. I'm glad today was good for you. Now you'd better get going! Your boss will be wondering where you are."

I watched as Hope hurried out the door, back to work. I was glad today had answered some questions for her. We needed to allow the biblical writings to be themselves. Reading them on their own terms was something we all needed to learn despite our post-Enlightenment confidence. I wondered what questions Hope would ask next time.

3 — What have we been worshipping all these centuries?

It was a couple of weeks before Hope texted again. When we were settled at *The Cup* with our coffees in front of us, she explained that work had been extra busy and time for thinking had been scarce.

"But I have done some thinking. I get that our mind-set now is different from the mind-set before The Enlightenment. That got me wondering about what we've been believing in the centuries since then. Is it accurate? Have we been worshipping a post-Enlightenment version of the real thing? And, if so, what distortions have crept in because we think so differently?"

"Another great question, Hope. All the greater because it gives me a chance to use a metaphor which is a pre-Enlightenment way of looking at religion. It's one that came to mind when I was trying to work this stuff out for myself."

I took a sip of coffee and, yes, grabbed a napkin and did my usual scramble in my bag for a pen.

"Remember that a metaphor tells the truth but not in a scientifically proven way. It may look historical, but it isn't quite 'historical' in the way we understand the term."

I drew a line and put tufts of grass along it.

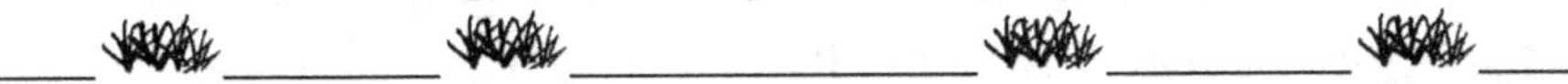

"Let's say this is the ground on which we stand. Some might call it real life. It is the concrete, material world. We know it well. It holds little mystery for us," I said. Hope nodded.

Underneath the ground I drew a stream of water running all the way across the napkin from one side to the other.

"Let's say the spirit of life is like an aquifer underneath the ground of our being. It runs inexhaustibly throughout the world, but underneath the surface of our lives. I've drawn it like a stream of water here. Being spirit, however, it is invisible. What frustrates scientists is that it's not measurable either, at least not with our usual scientific instruments. You need to just allow that it is there. You need to let it be something that is true in that different, metaphorical way which is the way of the spirit."

Hope nodded again, her face intent.

"Now, let's say the spirit has erupted into the real world at different times through the ages."

I drew a series of four fountains, springing up out of the aquifer. They burst through the ground along the length of the top line, at irregular intervals.

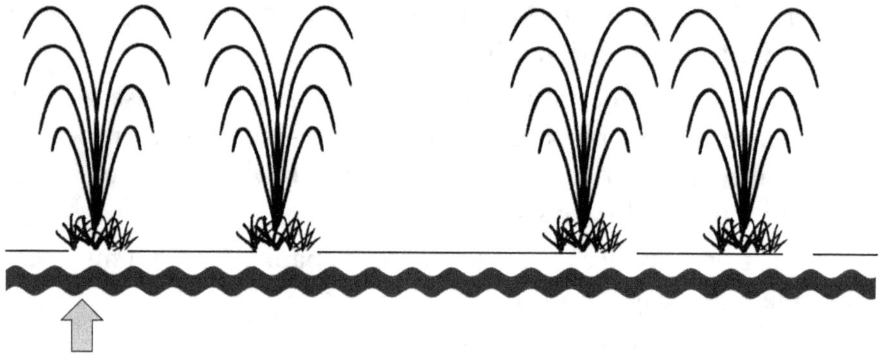

I pointed to the first fountain at the left-hand end of the line.

"Let's say this was the spirit erupting into the life of Abraham, a nomadic sheep and goat herder living in the Middle East, 2,000 years before Christ. Or it could be that time when a bush seemed to burn without being burnt up, attracting the attention of Moses who was tending his father in law's sheep in the desert of Midian. The spirit springs up, often unexpectedly in an individual's life, inspiring them to actions which are inexplicable to their peers. They begin a spiritual quest. Gradually, others may gather around them and follow their lead."

I move my pen to the next fountain.

"Let's say this fountain represents the special spirit which people recognised in Jesus when he lived and taught in Israel. His words seemed refreshing. They satisfied people's spiritual thirst. More and more gathered round him; his disciples, the crowd. After his death, more and more joined the growing movement which eventually became what we know as Christianity."

I move my pen to the next fountain. Hope breaks in. "That one might be Pentecost when the spirit changed the way the disciples saw Jesus' message."

"You could be right. We're playing with the metaphor here. Nothing is fixed or set in concrete. It's the idea we're pursuing. These fountains stand for any kind of major eruption of the spirit into the concrete world."

Hope nods. "This is cool."

My pen moves to the last fountain.

"And this one could be the spirit's impulse that energised St Francis or any of the great spiritual leaders who founded religious orders. It could be the spiritual impulses which led Luther to kick start the Reformation. In a world where religion had become stale and corrupt, these spiritual leaders discovered fresh sources of the spirit's power."

"I've only drawn four fountains here, but thank goodness, there have been many, many fountains pushing through the earthiness of our lives. Think of any great spiritual leader you know – they are an indication of the spirit's fountain activity."

I waved my pen over all the fountains. "This is all marvellous. Human beings in different epochs react to a direct experience of spirit. But a major problem is that the spirit is not a visible fountain of water. You can't put your hand into it, or drink directly from it. It is an invisible force. It affects people in different ways. No one can see it. What happens then when you try to explain what spirit is to people who didn't have the original experience? Or if you are speaking to those living later, after the beginnings of a spiritual movement? You need something to help people 'see' the way this invisible force might work."

Hope sipping her coffee, nodded. "Yes, I can see that is a problem. It still is. A lot of what's talked about in church is invisible. Not everyone gets it that easily."

"Did you ever watch the film *Hollow Man*? It might have come out when you were too young to watch it.[16] Kevin Bacon plays a scientist whose team invents an invisibility drug. (A bit like Harry

Potter's invisibility cloak.) Kevin Bacon's character takes increasing doses of the drug. When he's invisible, you can't see him unless he wears rubber gloves, a full face mask and clothes. The special effects were quite good. You could see just a hand moving in the air when he was wearing only a rubber glove on that hand and nothing else. It was cool."

"The concept that connects this to the aquifer metaphor is that something invisible needs a material expression for people to 'see' it," I said.

"I think I've seen a trailer of that movie, never got what it was about though," said Hope. "In the aquifer metaphor, do those experiencing spirit need to find the equivalent of Kevin Bacon's masks and gloves and clothing to make the spirit visible?"

"You've got it. Often, a religious movement will use rituals or ceremonies. Or they create material reminders of what this invisible force meant to them and how it changed their lives. Maybe at first in Abraham's case, it was the practice of circumcision. Maybe after the Exodus experience with Moses and Joshua, it was the Passover meal which later morphed into Christian communion. And, of course, all Christian artists aim to make spiritual reality visible." As I talked, I drew little diagrams of objects surrounding the fountains and 'clothing' them.

"For example, at Pentecost the symbols of fire and rushing wind became part of the pageantry. The colour red was reserved for the spirit. It's used on vestments and Pentecost day banners. This is to indicate that the spirit is seen as especially important on feast days and in ordination ceremonies. All of these are metaphorically 'clothing' the spirit to make it visible."

Hope is looking thoughtful again. I can tell she's had an 'aha' moment. She points to the symbols I've sketched. "There's a lot of this 'clothing' trying to make and keep the spirit visible in Christianity. You could include all the cathedrals, Gothic arches, stained glass windows, crosses, banners for the liturgical seasons in church…"

"That's right. And also hymns, creeds, the shape of the rituals, the sacraments… you can go on and on. Can you see any problems in this approach? Or how this could, with all the best intentions, go off-track?" I asked.

Hope looked at the napkin covered now in symbols and drawings. She was thinking deeply. After a while she spoke tentatively.

"The 'things' aren't actually the spirit, are they?" she asked slowly. "They represent the spirit, but they aren't it. For instance," she said, putting her finger on the chalice symbol, "maybe people think when they take communion that the meal itself is the important thing. They might miss connecting with the spiritual force it represents."

"That's right. Slowly, over centuries, more and more visible, tangible, concrete representations were amassed by the church. Followers had good spiritual experiences associated with these symbols. That meant in some cases they got overly attached to the objects present at the time. They spent more and more time, energy and money creating them, honouring them, and preserving them. It wouldn't be too strong a word to say they worshipped them," I said.

"They worshipped them… instead of the spirit?" Hope asked.

"Exactly. In some ways all those objects, even the Bible, can be idols if they take the place of the divine. That's if they become more important than the spirit itself. You know, I think you could say that the church as a whole – the Christendom church – has slipped, over the centuries, into worshipping the wrong thing. We have venerated external objects. You can see it very clearly when a particular church has to close (unfortunately quite common now). Members grieve the loss of stained glass windows, for example. There's protest and grief and argument as if the building were as important as God herself!"

"Is that why people get into arguments over things like what you can and can't do with the communion table? Or why they disagree on who's allowed to take communion? Is it why it's such a big thing that people believe every word in the creeds?" asked Hope.

"That's what I think," I replied. "The energy of devotion belongs to our relationship with the invisible spirit. It has become diverted, however, to visible symbols of spirit. Symbols have differing significance in the various denominations."

Hope sat back in her chair. She pushed her hand through her hair. "That makes sense! It means… it means a lot of stuff I've felt I had to do, or had to do a certain way, is only *relatively* important. What is really important is whether I have a connection with the invisible spirit. The vital thing is that I connect with the fountain."

"Yes. Of course," I said. "But making that connection with the spirit can be difficult. I try not to be dismissive of the intentions of the liturgists and artisans and faithful congregational members. They've created centuries of 'clothing' for the fountain of the spirit. I love a lot of what they created. They were trying to help a difficult process go better. Of course, many were inspired by genuine spiritual experiences but somewhere along the line, the focus changed."

I ran my pen along the line of the underground aquifer.

"When I read David Tacey's *Beyond Belief: Religion as Metaphor,* I thought that the aquifer of the spirit in my metaphor was the myth he talks about. Both run through all our religious impulses. It's what I think of when I talk about the Big Story."

"The Big Story is all about satisfying spiritual thirst. It's all about bringing life. It's about nurturing and growing the human being. It is all about the way real water helps plants, and therefore the whole planet, to grow and develop and interact. It's all about growing our inner but very human lives," I said.

"Water is to the planet as the spirit is to the soul. Water grows the planet as the spirit grows our inner life."

Hope grinned mischievously. "Are you sure the aquifer is water? Sure it's not coffee? Thanks a lot. Gotta go." And she was gone.

I chuckled and pushed aside the now cold coffee in my cup. Time for a reflective cup of tea.

As I drank my herbal infusion, I remembered another metaphor which had formed for me on my journey to understanding what on earth was going on with the church.

This metaphor also connected God with water. That wasn't surprising. Water fills the entire space available. It flows into any part of the world. It's the source of life. It maintains freshness and possibility in the world. Taking all those characteristics, it's a surprisingly good description of what we've called 'God' all these millennia.

In this metaphor, God is represented by the ocean. In this huge, vast, limitless ocean, over time, islands appeared. They were caused by volcanic eruptions from the floor of the ocean. They were like the fountains springing up from an underground aquifer. They resulted from divine-human interaction. Slowly, over centuries, many different islands formed in the wide ocean.

The various islands represent different religions of the world. There is an island where Christianity develops, another where Judaism forms, a third where Islam is the growing movement. Buddhism would have an island also, and Sikhism, Shinto, Hinduism and all the others. Even now, more islands are appearing in the ocean of Love that is God.

I remembered thinking about the activity on each island. The 'clothing' that Hope and I had talked about would be there. There are buildings like chapels, cathedrals, and churches. There are creeds and affirmations, confessions, and dogma. People use vestments and banners, rituals, and membership. All the 'clothing' reflects the islands' connection with the ocean around it.

The islands depend on the ocean for their existence. At the same time, however, strangely, they insulate their inhabitants *from* the ocean. You could live in your religion-island home all your life. You might never ever go to sea.[17]

I imagine people vary in their reaction to that possibility, as devotees in the real church do. Some remain inside the religious island community. Others are brave enough to occasionally visit the seaside. They enjoy these outings, paddling or even swimming not too far from shore. They like connecting with the ocean in a controlled way. Their spiritual batteries are recharged by such an experience.

Other, braver, souls might venture further out with the protection of sea-worthy craft like kayaks, surfboards, yachts or ocean-going vessels.

Then there are those who trained and practised. When they can, they successfully dive deep into the depths of the ocean. They come to know it more intimately. Those deep-sea divers are the mystics of our time.

Occasionally, people swim or sail far over the horizon. They become one with the vast ocean of love. They are celebrated by their communities as outstanding examples of how to be at one with God.

Sadly, the island communities can't adequately make this kind of connection for the majority of their people. Some repeat ancient stories of storms as dire warnings of the potential damage the ocean can cause to humans. Stories are told of shipwrecks at sea and lives lost. Others are always afraid of wrath-filled waves beating on the shoreline. They advocate renovating buildings with adequate shutters, and urge good damp proofing as barriers against the ocean.

There are leaders who fail to discourage misleading legends such as these. Like the story of what could happen if suddenly the ocean swamps an island. Might all the inhabitants drown in one final apocalyptic act? They re-tell this story though there is little evidence it will happen.

But every now and then, a person like Hope is born into the community. Someone who heard child-sized stories about the ocean. A little girl who paddled, swam, sailed and dived in it. When the stories no longer gave valid answers for her increasing questions, she searched further. She talked to the wise, weather-beaten members of the community. She read histories of surfers and the swimmers. She listened to sailors and deep-sea divers. She even made voyages to other islands observing island religions different to her own. She grew skilled in activities connecting her with the life and vigour of the ocean. Increasingly, she lived and moved and had her being in the ocean. She learned from her questions. She learned through new practices. As she matured into a different kind of faith, she knows there is nothing to fear from the ocean. Indeed, she finds in all her exploring that there is much to learn in its depths.

It is a delight to be asked to be one of the truth tellers in her explorations.

4 — If the Christian project is dying, what do I do now?

Texts and emails flew back and forth between Hope and me in the following week. I sent her the oceans metaphor. She asked several discerning questions. I got new ideas from her about developments on different islands which extended the image. Then Hope reminded me she was going on holiday the following week. She would not be in town for a café conversation. She booked a time, however, for when she was back, saying she was keen to continue talking.

The next Friday, Hope looked relaxed and tanned. A week at her parents' home seemed to have suited her. They'd retired to a seaside town. Visits to them were like mini holidays. I wondered if she'd talked with her now retired minister-turned-professor father about our conversations.

The business of queuing and ordering over, we settled into our usual booth. Miraculously, it was free on this busy morning. Hope fished part of a newspaper out of her bag. "Have you seen this?" she asked.

'This' was a feature article about the most recent census figures on religion. For the first time in the New Zealand's history, those ticking the 'No Religion' box were greater in number than Christians, previously the largest religious group in the country. The headline declared 'The Nones have it!'

"Yes, I have," I nodded. "It was predicted at the last census for next census. The speed of the change since then has caught people unawares."

"So, what's going to happen now?" asked Hope.

"What do you mean, 'what's going to happen?'" I asked.

"It says here the 'Nones' are mostly people my age and younger. What happens when all you oldies die out? The Christian 'thing' is going to die." Hope grinned and winked, acknowledging her relegation of me to 'oldie.'

"'The Rise of the Nones,' as they call it here, is already a huge sign the Christian 'thing' isn't working for a lot of people. Except, it says here, for charismatic and evangelical churches."

I nodded. "Research shows evangelical and charismatic churches tend to have big memberships. That research also shows that while many people join these churches, many people also leave at the same time. So that's not as hopeful as it looks either."

"It's true the Christian project isn't satisfying people as it used to," I continued. "There was a time when Christendom thrived and most people in Western society agreed with it. There was a consensus you could say."

I reached for the now inevitable napkin and drew a semicircle of bubbles with arrows reaching from them to a point at the top of the diagram where I drew a cross.

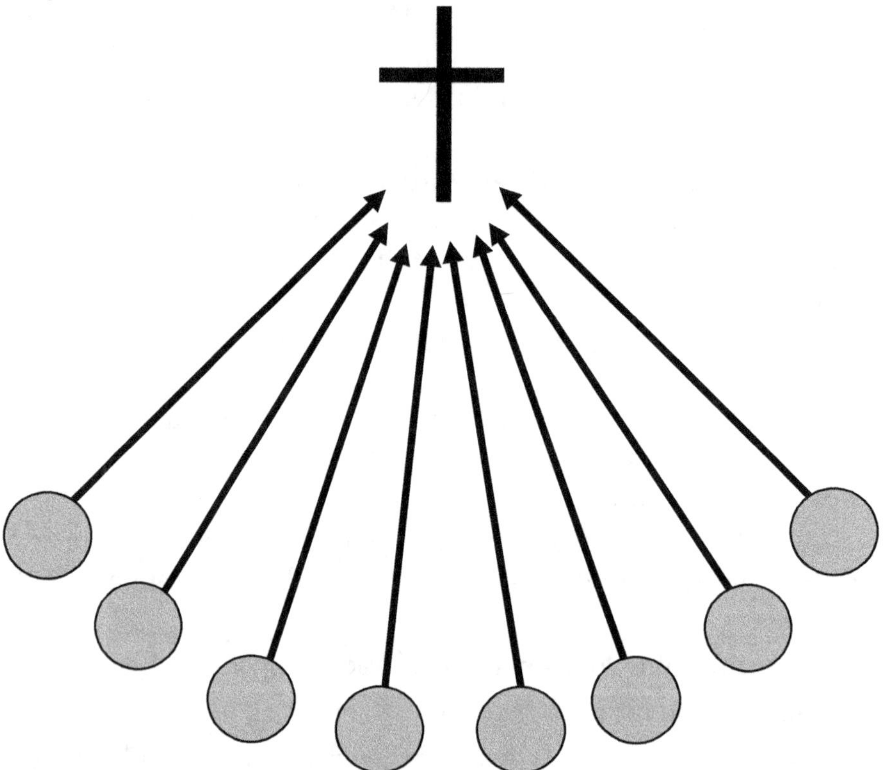

"This is a diagram I came across in a book by Edward Edinger, a Jungian analyst and writer.[18] It summed up what I'd been noticing but never put together. This is my simplified version."
"As a Jungian, Edinger is taking a psychological approach. He calls our connection to God a 'projection.' This means each person

gives what we call 'God' the characteristics and values we need in a superhero. Psychologically speaking, we 'project' on to the God-concept a whole scenario of what 'God' is like. During Christendom (the Middle Ages and the early Modern period we've been talking about) Church and State interacted as a kind of governing authority for all Western society, especially European society."

"During that time, Christian symbols and rituals were compatible with everyone's projections. It worked for a lot of people. You can see this kind of 'tepee,' or 'Big Top' shape (in the diagram) would be quite stable."

"But since the Enlightenment, Christianity's influence has crumbled. Religious symbols have lost their power. Consensus about their usefulness has fallen away. That's happened for individuals on their own faith journey, and for societies. People and communities of people are questioning religious faith assumptions more frequently."

"You could think of this as society growing out of the 'clothing.' Remember that 'clothing' of rituals and other paraphernalia makes the fountain of the spirit visible? It is that clothing which is becoming irrelevant and meaningless. Consequently, people pay less attention. They give less allegiance to the church and its rules, and they stop believing themselves to be religious."

"We've found this out a little too late. We've found now those symbols were not doing the job they were intended to do. They were not connecting people in a living way with spirit. If they had been, I think people would not have got bored with religion."

"Of course, it could also be true that those symbols still connect many people with the spirit now. However, as our culture has changed, new symbols are needed to make the spirit visible."

"It is also true that in this post-Enlightenment period people have been more prepared to say that Christianity and its symbols aren't working for them. They feel less obliged to continue the Christian compact as Christianity has less sway in western society."

Hope had been nodding her head as I talked and now, she broke in. "Since we've been talking in these café meetings, I've been watching more carefully in church. There are some moments where what happens in church helps me feel connected. There are other moments when ritual or words just get in the way."

"I know what you mean," I replied. "I've also learned to watch carefully. I look intently for the one moment when that connection might happen for me. What does it for you?"

Hope smiled wryly. "The processional hymn does, strangely enough. We are all standing singing. It doesn't matter what the hymn is. We stand, and the candle and Bible and minister come down the aisle between us all. It's all unfolding like a butterfly emerging from a chrysalis. Or it's like a stage curtain opening, ready for the drama to commence."

"That's interesting," I said. "Some people say that's a moment when the hierarchy of the church is too evident. It turns them off. It's great you find that special."

"And another is when the children run up the aisle to light the candle," she added. "There is such an irreverent eruption of joy and energy. I like the contrast."

"I like that moment too," I said.

"The contemporary reading often grabs me," continued Hope. "Poetry or just a shortish quote can have an arresting effect on me. I think it 'works' because it's been chosen to resonate with the theme. By the time the readings happen the theme is becoming obvious. The contemporary reading focuses it so acutely I sometimes find myself catching my breath."

"Do all those moments happen in every service?" I asked.

"No, sometimes there's nothing. At other times there are one or two special moments. Some days the kids are only plain noisy!" replied Hope.

We laugh together. Our church has a small but highly intelligent group of children from a diverse set of family constellations. It's unpredictable what's going to happen next during the children's time of the service.

Hope had been incredibly open. I wanted to be as open to her too.

"As I watched an advent carol service recorded in Trinity College, Cambridge last week, I noted my reactions. Some moments had the magic and surprise I associate with connecting with spirit. At other times, when the organ was thundering and I didn't know the carol they were singing, it was just a cacophony. It all seemed far too triumphal to be accurately anticipating the birth of a baby in a rough Middle Eastern stable."

"There was one beautiful moment, though, when the candles were being lit. The light slowly spread through the chapel as a soprano was reaching really high, beautiful notes. I found it very moving. I understood then why some people go to church only on Christmas Eve."

"It's a pity every day couldn't be a Christmas Eve. The church seems to get it right then," said Hope, nodding. She played the flute sometimes at special services. She was often responsible for connecting moments I'd experienced in church. I told her so and she flushed with pleasure.

A small silence fell as we each remembered the mystery of those moments.

"Another cup?" asked Hope, eventually. I nodded and she went to the counter.

I sat quietly, feeling sad. I spend many hours in church, preparing for church and talking with people about church. Yet collectively, we so often miss that moment of contact.

I remembered a friend's critique of my reflection on Jesus meeting the Samaritan woman at the well. I'd been fascinated with the actual Jacob's well, which is now absorbed into an Eastern Orthodox church, in the Palestinian city of Nablus in the West Bank. I spent time in the Sunday reflection on a sort of geography lesson. Bluntly, she said, I missed the point. The point of the story for her was the connection between the woman and Jesus. She described the non-judgmental way Jesus led up to the moment. She said that helped create the possibility of a real encounter. I remember she called the point of contact the 'I-Thou' moment. It is a concept of philosopher Martin Buber's[19] which she learned in psychotherapeutic training. I knew what she meant from my own experience in therapy as a client.

An I-Thou moment is an authentic connection where each person is truly present to the other. The connection creates an 'in-between' state. It makes the relationship bigger than the sum of the parts of the two people. A new entity, the 'I-Thou', is formed. In it, each person is an 'I', not an 'it.'

My friend's critique can apply to church as well. On so many occasions, I as a minister miss the opportunity to be completely present because I get side-tracked by other concerns. People coming to church services can also miss the opportunity to be fully present. What is going on in their lives outside or inside the church community often gets in the way.

Occasionally it happens. Those moments Hope and I had just been talking about were examples. The 'between' came into being for us and we felt fully met as human beings. In those moments we were helped to grow into our humanity more fully. I remember an article which discussed 'I-Thou' in the context of counselling:

> Buber described the between as a bold leap into the experience of the other while simultaneously being transparent, present and accessible. He used the term "inclusion" to describe this heightened form of empathy. It is a far cry from the now-familiar scene of a group of friends sitting around a table at a restaurant, all gazing into their smartphones.[20]

I looked around and did a swift count. I could see ten pairs of people. In eight of them, both people in the pair were absorbed in their cell phones. I remembered vividly one other sentence in the article.

> Buber saw the meeting between I and Thou as the most important aspect of human experience because it is in relationship that we become fully human.[21]

That encapsulates for me the importance of connection and relationship in churches. Hopefully people can connect there with each other, and with God, and so become more fully human. What an opportunity! One which Hope's generation, and those younger, look for but fail to find in the contemporary church format. Are they 'talking past' each other? Is the church not 'present'? Or are they not 'present'? Or maybe, both are absent from the encounter?

Generation X and younger find the 'I-Thou' to some extent in the epic movies that have made their way into popular culture in recent decades. They espouse *Star Wars* as 'their' narrative, and many Gen Xers I meet comment on life and feelings via *Star Wars* references. For me, '*May the Force be with you,*' resonates with the ancient farewell, '*Go with God.*' I wonder if Gen Xers know that the core theme of *Star Wars* is good struggling with evil. Do they know it is the same myth running through the boring old Bible their grandparents revered!

The *Lord of the Rings* trilogy packed theatres. In New Zealand, it spawned a whole tourist industry as people sought the 'magical' filming locations. I wonder whether these movie-tourists long for a Fellowship of the Ring to accompany them on their life quests? Have they noticed the conversation about story in the trilogy. It was a connecting moment for me when Sam and Frodo pondered their fearful journey ahead into Mordor.

Sam talks to Frodo about not having started their quest if he'd known at the beginning all of what the journey would include. He muses about how characters in well-loved epic stories didn't turn back when the going got hard. They continued on because they believed there was still some good in the world worth fighting for. Frodo agrees with Sam that when you are in really important journeys, you don't know the end. He adds that is the best way to be.[22]

Just a few changes, and that could be a speech John might have given the disciples on Easter Saturday. Then they would have been better prepared for the next day and its startling events.

Tolkien knew he was writing a story which aligns with The Big Story, just as Christianity also aligns with that Story. I believe all our small stories align with the Great Myth/Big Story running through all our lives and societies. Tolkien has Frodo and Sam musing about stories and the characters in them. They talk about the roles of different individuals in the same kind of quest they are on.

Sam wonders aloud if Frodo, the hero, will feature in any of these epics? Frodo laughs and demurs, saying the story should also tell the part played by Samwise the Brave! Sam thinks he's joking, but Frodo is sincere.[23]

We don't always realise our own courage. We forget that even the great stories have their quiet, unseen moments. In ways hidden from others, our hearts experience personal pain, loneliness, and fear. Yet, we still keep going on the journey. Then of course Harry Potter…. my reverie was broken by Hope's arrival back at the table.

"Sorry about that, an enormous queue formed just as I got there. Everyone seemed to be confused about their order. Goodness knows when our coffee will arrive." Just as she finished speaking, the waiter delivered two flat whites. The delay was in the kitchen, not with the barista, apparently. Good job!

"We got to the breakdown of Christendom," said Hope. "What happens next?"

"That's the 64 million-dollar question!" I said, reaching for another napkin. At the top I drew the cross from the previous diagram broken in pieces.

"We know the symbols are broken for people who are stage four questioners or generations of your age and younger. Let's just look at five possible representative reactions." I drew five circles at the bottom.

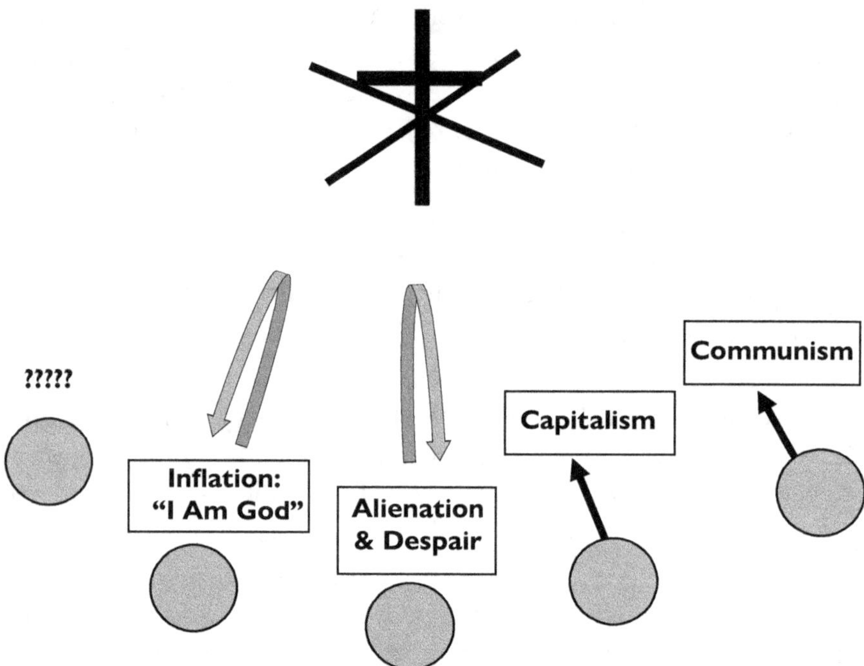

"Remember in Edinger's other diagram they were connected to the Christian symbols by straight lines? Well, now those projections must find another object. Or do they?"

"In four different scenarios, the person continues projecting or wishing to project their aspirations. Some look outwards. They find what becomes a new religion. They start to project their hopes and dreams on to that ideology. Capitalism and Communism are two contrasting ideologies. They are examples of what can become the 'new' religion for some people. They replace the former 'God' they worshipped who is now, for them, no longer relevant or reliable."

"Two other scenarios are where people still want to project on to something. They don't pick an outer ideology. When the Christian 'God' disappears for them as an object of worship, these two types of people project inwards. One inward projection results in despair and alienation as the person loses hope in being 'saved,' 'fixed' or 'rescued' by a Messiah figure. This can be mental ill health and suicide territory."

"The other results in what psychologists call inflation, as the person *becomes* 'God' themselves. These people have what we call over-inflated egos. Sometimes they are narcissistic personalities. President Trump was a particularly good example of this dynamic."

"The fifth and final scenario," I said pointing to the circle at the far left, "is where the person looks within themselves. This is not to find *they* are a domineering, autocratic God. It is to find the centre within them where the spirit dwells in the Self."

"This movement is familiar to Jung's followers. Everyone maintains a false self every day to get through life. It's called the persona. You can think of it like a mask you wear to a masquerade or a fancy-dress party. The mask helps you project out into the world a certain image or character. Sometimes it is close to what is inside you and sometimes it can be quite different."

"For instance, the bright, extroverted youth leader may inside be an introverted personality. The helpful, cheerful bookshop assistant might be a grumpy bear of a person at home," I added, grinning at Hope across the table.

"How did you know?" she asked, also grinning.

"I get the replacement of God with other ideologies," she said, pointing at the communism and capitalism boxes.

"I think I've also seen some examples of these other two. You're right, Trump does think of himself as omnipotent and the centre of the universe. I've certainly known some depressed and alienated students in my time at uni. I meet them in the bookshop, too. My Dad was depressed for a while as he was changing his theology. I wonder if that connects with this diagram. I'll have to think about that."

"Did you notice that when you were home?" I asked carefully.

Hope didn't talk much about her parents.

"Mmmm," said Hope but didn't seem to be inclined to expand on her comment.

Instead, she tapped on the circle with no arrows leading out from it. "Tell me the detail of what happens here?" she asked, then noticed her watch. "Oh my gosh! Gotta go." She scrambled her gear together and was gone.

"Bye!" I raised my hand in farewell. Perhaps it was just as well to have a break. That was a big question Hope had just asked. We might need fresh minds to tackle it.

5 — The emperor's clothing is seductive: can I let it go?

Hope was clear at our next meeting at *The Cup* that the options I'd described from Edinger's diagram so far weren't ones she wanted to follow.

She didn't want to fall into the trap of replacing the Christian story with another ideology such as communism or capitalism or any other ideology roaming the world wide web.

She thought believing herself some godlike creature wasn't her thing either.

She admitted to some fear and occasional depression over the questions bothering her. But she didn't feel she was falling into despair, "As yet," she added with a grin.

"In fact," she said, smiling at me shyly, "these conversations have really helped with that. I'm sure now there *is* a journey, and I *am* on it. These conversations have given me frameworks for understanding where I am. They've also reassured me there are others walking the same path. Some have even written books I can read. Also, I now know why some people aren't on the same route. That's their journey. It doesn't have to be mine. That clarity is really helpful."

"Good," I murmured quietly, while my heart turned mad cartwheels of joy.

"I remember you said we don't always get full answers to our questions. But I want to ask about this option here," she continued. Producing last session's napkin, she pointed to the unlabelled circle on the left of the diagram.

"This is where getting definite answers becomes an impossible quest," I replied wryly. "This kind of person," I said, tapping the circle she'd indicated, "realises that looking *outside* yourself isn't the answer."

"It's a bit like the story of the Emperor's new clothes. Most of the crowd are content to go along with the majority opinion. They're happy to live over-inflated lives," I said, tapping the next circle. "Or they don't think there is a way out of their despair," I added, tapping that circle. "Or they keep their minds by becoming busy with causes," I finished, moving my finger to the communist and capitalist circles.

"But, some people, usually a minority, like the little boy in the Emperor's new clothes story, see through the Group Think. They know, (if I can put it like this), that the emperor's new clothing is inadequate. They know that the 'clothing' the church places around the essential spirit in those aquifer-fed fountains is inadequate. And (if I can twist the emperor's new clothes story to a meaning it didn't originally have!), they realise you need to stand naked, without pretence, before the truth for it to set you free."

"Kahlil Gibran has a question like that in his poem on Death," said Hope. She quoted:

> "For what is it to die but to stand naked in the wind
> and to melt into the sun?" [24]

"Mmmm, that does connect. In a sense this whole faith transition is about letting old ideas die."

"A requirement for this position," I said, tapping the unnamed circle, "*is* a degree of being stripped of old assumptions, beliefs, and habits. It is difficult to persist in this position. It's a minority position. Perhaps one in ten people hear this call and answer it. When you are used to being in the majority, it is disconcerting to find yourself in the minority. It can be a lonely journey."

"Jung called this movement to change your direction the 'Second Invitation.' He sees it as moving into a deeper inner life than we lived in the first part of life. In a way, Jung is talking about a two stage 'faith' process. His terms for it would be first invitation/second invitation. It's not unlike Borg and Moore using three stages of faith."

Hope nodded; her eyes focused on the diagram.

"You might choose to go with this type of reaction," I said, tapping the unlabelled circle again, "You would be choosing to enter the disenchantment process fully. Then you may eventually find re-enchantment. Each writer or thinker uses different terms. They talk about it differently because of their varying backgrounds. I think it is really all the same process."

"The people we've been talking about come at it from their different theological, psychological, sociological, educational backgrounds. The actual process in which real people find themselves is all those things. It's about our personal theology, our psychology and our social processes. It certainly is educational. But, not at all like school as we knew it!"

Hope laughed with me.

"By accepting this invitation to go deeper, what you're doing is volunteering to go behind the persona I talked about last week. Remember the persona; that mask we all show people; the person we want others to think of us as. Behind the persona is the depth of your Self with a capital S. This isn't what others might call selfish with a small 's.' The Self is the inner, essential you."

"It's not your ego. The ego organises your life. It sometimes bosses you about a bit to get what it wants. What's the process behind accepting the second invitation or wrestling with disenchantment? It's the process of quietly and firmly de-throning the ego. It's getting to know the Self better. It takes a while. It's surprising what you find out about yourself in that process."

"I think I get what you are talking about," replied Hope. "I'm sure I've only a hazy idea of what it all means yet. The idea of going deeper attracts me in a quite persistent way, though. I have a feeling of 'coming home.' It's a feeling about being truly myself, not a 'Great Pretender.'" She paused. "But this is also where you were saying we don't always get straight answers to all our questions?"

"Yes," I replied. "That deep-inside-feeling you're on the right track is all the certainty you get. Some days, even that's a bit wobbly! Religious belief systems, creeds and confessional statements are black and white and secure. This different way is uncertain and mysterious. It's completely *unlike* the certainty offered by ancient church documents."

Hope nods thoughtfully. "What triggers people into this second journey?"

"Various events. There's a whole bunch of examples in the Bible. That story when Abraham almost sacrifices Isaac, (which seems so weird to us), is a turning point for him. Jacob's night spent wrestling with the angel changes the way he lives his life. Moses' moment at the burning bush is another epiphany which changes his life-course. Joseph being sold to traders by his brothers meant he had to look at life completely differently. In the Second Testament the famous example is Paul's experience on the road to Damascus, which is so important that it's told three times in Acts."

"There are characters in the Bible who give away the opportunity when they have it. Esau, Lot and King Saul are examples of that. In the Second Testament, there's the rich young ruler who turns away from Jesus' challenge. Judas betrays Jesus instead of continuing to follow. Later in the book of Acts, Ananias and Saphira break the rules of the community. Who knows what all their lives would have been like if they had grasped the moment?"

"*Carpe diem*," murmured Hope.

"Exactly, *carpe diem*. There's one important characteristic of this different world. It's that it is about myth and mystery rather than firm beliefs and facts. That's why it seems less certain. The concepts you're dealing with are metaphorical and mythological, not historical and rational. Dave Tomlinson would say it was spoken in night language, as opposed to day language."[25]

"And not everyone understands that language," said Hope with a wry smile. I can tell she's thinking of people she knows well.

"No. It's like going to another country and speaking a different language. In the new language some words don't completely translate back into your first language and vice versa. The different world is described in terms new to you, but which suit the other culture you have entered."

"The metaphor of the aquifer and the fountains is a good example. Someone on the Second Journey 'knows' what is meant by that metaphor. They do not always need a detailed explanation or coding system. It is a *suggestion* of how complex a situation might actually be. It is not a precise blueprint relying on empirical proof or historical accuracy."

"It makes me think of how many different words the Inuit people have for snow. Snow makes up such a large part of their surroundings and lifestyle. For us, snow is less important, so we use fewer words for it," said Hope.

I smile at her. "Apparently, that was thought once to be an urban myth, but has actually been proven true recently if you take the languages of all the Inuit subtribes into account. There would also be things Inuit would not have any words for because they'd never known them. Remind me to tell you some time about Inuit children and IQ tests imported from southern Canada!"

We decide it's time for a break and our second cups of coffee. The shop has filled up and getting served is something of a trial. Perhaps, we decide, we should order two coffees at the beginning and get them to bring us one automatically halfway through.

"So where are you at with all this, Hope?" I dare to ask. "You originally came to me with a query about applying for the ministry. Does this resonate with that process at all or is that now irrelevant?"

"Yes and no!" smiled Hope. "In a way, I think I have been on the second journey for a while. But, I still don't know much about it. I don't know if I can or will begin to feel re-enchantment happening. I do feel much more—as if I 'have' something spiritually. Whatever that something is." She paused in thought.

"There's one connection I still have to make. It would make a difference in deciding whether I start the application process. It's how does this new path relate to the regular Christian one I was on before. Does this new 'knowing' relate to Christian Belief (with a capital B), its creeds, confessions and propositions?"

"I'm attracted to the idea of myth, (I've read some stuff about myth in books we have at the bookshop). But how does that relate to the Christian story the church follows? Dad never used the word 'myth' as a serious term when he was preaching, whatever stage his theology was at. First time round he didn't tell us that the history of biblical stories was unimportant. He often spent time explaining how stories in the Bible had *happened* at a particular time and how we could know that for sure. Latterly he was sure nothing was valuable. Do I throw all that away to follow this new idea of myth or are they still connected?"

"They are connected and yet they are very different," I replied. I saw the expression on Hope's face. "Sorry, this is where the answers become more uncertain than definite ones you're given in some churches."

I continued. "The connection is that both your new second journey and the Christian narrative are founded on the same basic myth. We could call that the Great Myth. It's not a single, distinct meta-narrative prescribed in exact detail for everyone. This Myth is about everyone's journey to becoming fully human. It's about the interplay of good and evil in the world and our lives. It's about the essence of our very Self. It's about how that essence has sparks of the divine within it. Bishop John Spong said,

> …when we become fully human, then we share in the very meaning of God. It means that we live with God's Life, and we love with God's Love and we are with God's Being.[26]

"That's what you are seeking as you look within to find the true Self that Jung writes about," I said.

"That, I believe, is also the core of the Christian narrative. Remember the aquifer metaphor? Think of that aquifer as not just spirit but also the Great Myth. As the fountains burst to the surface, they bring the Great Myth into the real world."

"Remember we said the 'clothing' human beings put on obscures the spirit? Well, it has also obscured the Great Myth. People end up treating the clothing and rituals as more important than the Great Myth. They believe their small 'm' myth religion is the only true and reliable myth around."

"Does this only apply to Christianity?" asked Hope. "Didn't Judaism and Islam also begin with something like one of those fountains of spirit bursting into the world?"

I nodded. "This might be where I part company with others who see Christianity as the best and only religion, but I agree with you. I see the same enchantment, disenchantment and re-enchantment process in followers of Judaism and Islam. As Jewish and Islamic people participate in Western education systems, they also take on board the Enlightenment mindset. The rise in their critical thinking can lead to disenchantment with their traditional religion."

"Like you, if no one is around to describe what is happening to them, they can think this means they have to throw out what they now see as an old-fashioned belief system. But many in Judaism and Islam can see a broader way into the future. I haven't talked much about Judaism and Islam in our conversations. It's not that I think they are worthless or inferior to Christianity. It's just I'm not expert in those religions, so I hesitate to speak for or about them."

Hope nodded. "The theory seems to make sense, though," she said. "I guess there is the same danger, as with Christianity, that former followers of Judaism or Islam throw it all away and become permanently atheist or humanist. Then those religions would experience the same decline as Christianity in some areas of the planet."

I nod again. "The difficulty with the uncertainty and mystery and mythic base of the re-enchantment process is that while many people understand the flow of what happens and can feel their own 'progress' in their spiritual lives, there are few resources for pursuing this process."

"There are a number of authors who in their different ways, from varying perspectives, have written about this awakening or reorientation. One of the first I read was Sue Monk Kidd, though her journey, as she writes it, might appeal to women rather than men.[27] She was raised a Southern Baptist and her journey would appeal to women from that kind of background."

"I've found Brian McLaren really useful – he particularly writes for evangelicals who are asking questions. The three books of his which I particularly enjoyed form a trilogy of novels about an evangelical pastor's crisis of faith and his conversations with a friend – some of them in coffee shops![28] He's also written about movements in theology.[29] As well, he's tackled the concept of spiritual practice for now."[30]

"He's been a leader in the emerging church which is a kind of a reinvention of the evangelical part of the American church, though the movement has international connections through the internet. That's a movement worth looking up and following. They have a website called *the emergent village*." Hope noted down McLaren's name and the website title.

"Another female writer with wide appeal is Karen Armstrong. She was a nun who left her order[31] and has written prolifically since.[32] Barbara Brown Taylor's dealt with this area in her *Altar in the World* and *Leaving the Church* and other books she's written since then.[33] Her writing's extremely easy to read. Lillian Daniel is also an interesting preacher and author."

"A couple more authors I've enjoyed are Dave Tomlinson[34] and Rob Bell,[35] a Brit and an American. They've a light touch, yet both think deeply. I like their inclusive acceptance of where people are at.

Dave Tomlinson has been leading a weekly YouTube session, called *The Holy Shed*, since the pandemic started in 2020 which is cool to watch. They both have an easy, contemporary style."

"Easy to read is good!" says Hope, with a twinkle in her eye, writing furiously.

"I've already mentioned Marcus Borg and John Dominic Crossan," I continued. "They've spent a lot of time with biblical questions in their books. They've been presenters on several DVDs for a group called Living the Questions, based on their trips to the Middle East which debunk some urban myths about the early Christian experience after Jesus' death. You'd enjoy the Living the Questions programmes."

"And, while Bishop John Spong wasn't a key part of my journey, others I know have really appreciated his approach."

"What about that guy Edinger from whom you got the 'tepee' diagram?" Hope asked. "What's he written?"

"Edward Edinger has quite a few books[36] where he interprets biblical material from a Jungian perspective, though you need to know something about Jungian thought to make real sense of all he writes. I stumbled through it a bit, but I got the gist well enough for them to be helpful. I can lend you some of these books I'm talking about. Just let me know what you'd like."

"That would be great," replied Hope. "My budget's all tied up with my travel plans for next year, so borrowing books would help."

"A rather hefty read is Cynthia Bourgeault, but she brings out the symbolic meaning within the Christian narrative. Her latest book is *Eye of the Heart,* and it delves into what she calls the imaginal realm, which is that interior consciousness I've been trying to describe – perhaps not too well.[37] Is all this making your eyes glaze over?" I asked.

"No!" said Hope who was still looking interested. "It's great to know all this writing exists. Can you email me a sort of booklist from these writers? I suppose they all have websites or blogs and things?"

"Yeah, sure! I'll group them approximately in the order I read them. That will give you a kind of progression of thought for yourself and through their development. Some do have websites or blogs. I can send you some links."

"Fantastic! Thanks again. I'll need to push off now, but this has been a great session." Hope gathered her stuff and was through the door with a rush of cool air.

Summer was ending but I had an idea that spiritually she was walking into a new Spring. I savoured the moment. I loved seeing people finding their feet on this rocky path to their true selves. I wondered what she would ask me next time.

6 — The Big Story behind the little old stories

At *The Cup* the following Monday, Hope looked a little bug-eyed. "Had a hard weekend?" I joked.

"Too right!" she replied, "I watched all of the Lord of the Rings movies in a binge marathon with my flatmates and Charlie."

"Really!" I exclaimed, as I used payWave to pay for our drinks. She was having an Americano. Perhaps it was to counteract the sleep-deprived weekend. I ordered tea as I'd had a couple of coffees already that day and was feeling a little wired.

Watching *Lord of the Rings* was an interesting move for Hope. Despite being a bookshop assistant, she veered towards non-fiction literature mostly. I hadn't known her to be very keen on the fantasy genre of movies. New Zealand felt it 'owned' the LOTR franchise, but I knew Hope had boasted of never having seen the trilogy.

"What brought that on?" I asked as we settled at our usual table. Being a Monday afternoon, the place was quiet for once.

"My flatmate Jason said I hadn't lived unless I'd seen all three movies," replied Hope with a yawn. "Even though it meant I went short of sleep I have to say I agree with him now. It was inspiring. A great mixture of the humble little hobbits and the warrior types who joined them in the Fellowship of the Ring. The huge battle scenes were a little much, though the special effects were great. I have to admit I found the whole thing quite gripping."

"That's neat," I replied and went on. "Now you think about it, without the movie actually happening right in front of you, what themes do you think were running through the action?"

Hope yawned again and fell upon her Americano which the server brought to the table, taking a sip immediately though it was too hot to drink yet. "Let me see. There was obviously a good and evil theme running through it all. The 'goodies' were small and outnumbered, but they prevailed in the end. There were some sacrifices, like Faramir leading his small cavalry troop into inevitable failure."

"Did Gandalf's story remind you of anyone?"

"Gandalf? He died and then came back as a spirit, didn't he?"

pondered Hope "He was sent back to Middle-earth to complete his mission, as Gandalf the White. Oh! I suppose that's like Jesus being resurrected in the Bible!"

"Yes, and I always thought there was a resonance between Frodo having the burden of carrying the Ring and Jesus carrying the Cross," I said. "A lot of temptation for both of them not to go through really hard parts of the journey. Both were tempted to take the easy route dangled in front of them."

"Of course! I hadn't put that together. It was a big responsibility for them," said Hope.

"When Frodo thanks Sam for his support and loyalty. Sam could be thought of as what the Bible would call a follower or a disciple. The Fellowship of the Ring could kind of stand for the whole group of disciples, both when Jesus was alive and the larger groups which formed in the Early Church," I said.

"So," said Hope slowly, counting off on her fingers, "in the *Lord of the Rings* movies there are themes which are also in the Bible. There's the battle between good and evil. There's the idea of making a dangerous, risky journey when you don't know the way completely ahead of time. There's the idea of a leader doing the hard thing, and companions helping with the task."

"The whole thing is a quest, isn't it, just as Jesus was on a quest to establish what being fully human was like and urged people to go on that quest with him. There's the idea you can be tempted away from your main task. And there's the idea that the goal is so important you might have to give your life for it."

"And," I added, "there's the idea that to do this Big Thing and follow this Big Story, your own little story of living in the Shire (which once was your whole world and seemed everything to you); becomes unimportant compared with risking it all for what your heart now says you need to do."

"And," added Hope in her turn, "in the process you have to reach deep inside yourself for reserves of strength you didn't know you had. You get to know yourself much, much better than you knew yourself living quietly at home in the Shire."

"That's right," I said. "The quest to deliver the ring or to carry the cross isn't really about the ring or the cross. If we make it about the ring or the cross, we're turning them into magical objects. On the contrary, the quest is about what you learn about yourself on the journey. It's about how you mature in your way of looking at yourself and how you begin to understand on a new level how you deal with other people. That is what is meant by finding the God/god within. You delve down into those reserves of strength you didn't know you had and find there the support you need."

"It reminds me of a piece I wrote for Storm Sunday one year. It was an interpretation of the story of the storm on the lake. I can send it to you. The gist of it was that the Jesus figure sleeping in the boat wasn't merely a real-life Jesus. That Jesus character in the story can represent our inner resources, our sleeping Self. It's that part of us we have not been conscious of until now."

"During the storm, which represents any crazy life-crisis which tosses us about, we are driven to wake up and use resources we didn't acknowledge we had before. It is not about the disciples waking up Jesus to help them as an external support. It is we who wake up to the resources within ourselves. The difference between the storm before we wake up and the calmness we feel after we wake up is stunning and awe inspiring. It's just like the awe the disciples feel in the story, that this is a numinous, holy moment. In the same way we can have many numinous, holy moments as we make more and more discoveries about ourselves on this mythical journey."

"Wow," breathed Hope, her eyes round, "I feel like Samwise walking outside the Shire for the first time and discovering a whole new world. That story was one which bugged me most in the bible. It seemed so unlikely to be true … in an Enlightenment sense, I mean," she added hastily.

"I think you'll find if you and your flatmates binge watch the *Star Wars* series, and the *Harry Potter* movies, there's the same resonance."

I continued, "I don't know whether to worry that younger generations who haven't been to Sunday School, don't know that the themes in the movies which they love and re-watch and quote all the time, are in the Bible, or just be glad they are experiencing those themes. Movies are so much more alive and colourful and engaging. It's easier to absorb the drama and the power of the spirit in those myths than reading bible stories in obscure, stiff, formal language or listening to audio-only sermons or reflections."

"While sitting on a hard pew with no popcorn!" laughed Hope.

"Yeah, right!" I laughed too, mostly at what the older generation might think of popcorn in church. That reminded me of what church used to be like when I was a teenager.

"The sad thing, as I look back, is that the great myths in the Bible didn't get used well – or sometimes not at all – while others took centre stage all the time. For instance, the emphasis on needing to be saved," I said.

"In my church's case, you needed to be saved from Hell because right from birth you were considered a sinner. It was a very dualistic approach. There were only good and bad people and both heaven and hell were already designated; heaven was for the good and hell was for the bad. God had the final say apparently. This was tied to Jesus' death."

"To explain the significance of his death the biblical writers used the old Jewish myth of the scapegoat. Each year on the Day of Atonement, a Jewish village would choose an animal and set it off into the desert, believing it carried all the sins of the village. It was the scapegoat for them all. When the disciples were pondering why Jesus had died, it would have been natural for them to turn to their own well known stories. So, they saw Jesus as the scapegoat for all the world, not just a village."

"I was taught that what we had to do was accept him as our particular scapegoat and we would be free (and therefore good and suitable for heaven)."

"It was an inspiring story for people who felt caught in a never-ending cycle of failure and hopelessness. But it meant that other ways in which we needed to be freed or liberated were pushed aside in favour of one dominant myth – the substitutionary atonement story."

"Hmm," Hope nodded her head. "'Greater love has no one than this, than to lay down one's life for their friends.'"[38]

"Yes," I nodded back. "It was Marcus Borg who helped me see there were other myths which described how we might be liberated in a variety of ways. They don't focus only on wrongdoing. He had about six, I think. The three that made the most impression on me were, the Exodus, which was about freedom from bondage, the Exile, which was about coming home after estrangement and the third was bringing of light to the blind."

Hope looked interested in this turn of the conversation. "Being set free from bondage in an Exodus experience could be getting free of addictions, or old habits, or prejudice, or conforming when you shouldn't – there's loads of things we might need to be freed from which could be like slavery in Egypt."

"Exactly," I replied, "The Exile was an experience hundreds of years before Christ in which the Jewish people got captured and taken into exile by the Babylonians. Three generations later, when the Persians invaded Babylon, the Jewish people were freed and allowed to go home. There are lots of times in our lives when we wander off the path or get distracted or get carried away by others. It's a good feeling to come home and realise love's always there waiting for you."

"That sounds very like the prodigal son story," said Hope. "I guess the seeing light after being blind myth is based on the blind man Jesus is said to have healed."

"Yes," I replied, "we can be in the dark about a lot of things. I talked before about being asleep in the boat. Recovery of sight for the blind could be a version of that waking up to being conscious of what we have been doing. Or it could be that we have been deliberately kept in the dark and need our eyes to be opened. Or it could be damage from way back which is preventing us seeing the truth."

Hope nodded thoughtfully. I could see the ideas taking hold. "Those ideas all give a lot more room to move than only using the trad atonement theory," she said. "He lists more too?"

"Yes, it's all in a chapter on Salvation in Borg's book *Convictions*. It's not that the atonement theory doesn't still have mileage for us. We all do wrong from time to time and need to take responsibility for that and ask forgiveness. The atonement model is good for that. Focusing on sin only, however, has the unfortunate effect of labelling us too thoroughly as bad people. There are other more subtle issues which we need to sort-out, where we haven't necessarily sinned, but do need help to live better as human beings. Concentrating only on sin can mean we miss a chance to develop further.

Spong would say,

> … the role of the church is not to rescue the sinners, but to empower people to become more fully human."[39]

"Today's had a heap of stuff in it," said Hope, reaching for her bag. "Who would have thought a binge movie session could have led to all this! I've been thinking about applying for ministry training by the way, and I've lots of questions about what it is like for women to train and to be a minister. Also, all those big church rituals we do like baptism, confirmation and communion. Where do they fit into this different perspective?"

"You certainly keep me busy, Hope," I laughed. "Go well."

She was out the door.

7 — Who or what is God in the world of myth and mystery?

I reflected on Hope's final comment about ministry applications and church rituals. There was a larger matter to discuss first, before we got into the meaning of Christian rituals. Who or what was 'God' in the re-enchanted world of myth and mystery? I texted her.

> Me: Hope, have been thinking. Before church rituals, what about God?

> Hope: God, or 'God'? Like the word or not?

> Me: Hmm. Christendom's 'God' was a personal deity who intervenes.

> Hope: That why people r alwys praying 2 God 4 things?

> Me: Exactly. Relief from suffring, cures, for a mate, etc.

> Hope: Both Allies & Germans prayed 4 God 2 b on their side, WW II.

> Me: People expect a lot from a personal deity.

I wondered where to go from here. The pandemic? The 2020-21 global pandemic is an affront to this understanding of God. Is God angry with the world? Is this our punishment, like the First Testament plagues visited on the Egyptian population? If God is compassionate, why are so many people dying? Why doesn't God step in? Climate change is advancing. Why doesn't God stem natural disasters? Why does God allow people to be robbed of their land by erosion? Did God think it's OK for them to lose homes through flooding and forest fires?

> Me: Covid-19 is a problem for that kind of belief.

> Hope: Yes. My uncle Tom left church cos of it. Reckons God's a crock cos he isn't acting.

I wondered again where to go next. Theists, deists and atheists take varying views. Deism is belief in a god, but their god is impersonal. Deists believe god to be the creator and overseer of the universe. They don't believe that god wants to have a personal relationship with humankind. A deist might wonder about why a god who creates and oversees the universe, allows a lot of suffering and pain. At least, they don't believe that god cares about human beings in the first place.

Theists believe God or gods seek a personal relationship with all or some human beings. Uncontrollable events happen on earth like earthquake, fire, pandemic or flood. It's more difficult to reconcile that with a God who cares. Shouldn't God care when human beings are struck by poverty, famine, disease and death?

John Spong's comment about this dichotomy popped into my mind:

> … Christianity has got to redefine itself in terms of this new world. Copernicus, Kepler and Galileo destroyed the dwelling place of God above the sky, and in effect the theistic definition of God with it. After the destruction of this God, we've got to find a new way of talking about God beyond theism. The only alternative to theism that our world seems to know is atheism. We've got to find a way of getting beyond that opposition. We've got to find a new way of talking about God.[40]

• • •

Me: Know the diff btwn theism and deism?

Hope: In deism God doesn't intervene; in theism God does?

Me: Yes. Pandemics r easier on deists than theists. They don't expect God to care.

Hope: Atheism?

Me: Pop view is atheists don't believe God. But it can be written 'a-theist.'

Hope: What's the diff?

Me: Not believing in a personal God but being deist or having a gen belief in spirituality.

Hope: Flatmate's home. I'm cooking. Email me more?

Me: Sure.

That evening I emailed her about where my thoughts were heading. Once I got started, one thing led to another and another. Hope and I had quite the internet conversation during the next few days.

Hi Hope,

Moving on from today's texting:

(Please take inverted speech marks round the word God as read)

Whether God intervenes in human lives has caused angst for centuries in Christianity. Views vary as much as the billions of Christians worldwide. God's performance/non-performance on natural disasters can be a major faith crisis, especially for those raised to believe a powerful personal God loves you and wishes you good.

What's more, we equate 'our' God usually only with pleasant circumstances. We assume it's God when we recover from illness. We think it is God who has helped us be successful. It's good of God to help us evade serious bereavement (at least until old age). It's God who beautifully nurtures our spirit.

We don't want to think that illnesses we can't explain, sudden flooding ruining homes or earthquakes might be 'acts of God' (as insurance companies call it). We don't realise our character is honed/refined when we live through difficulties. Sometimes we learn more from them, than from the pleasant and comfortable aspects of our lives. A paradox. It's hard to grasp.

The Christianity in which I was raised taught God was personal. 'He' was definitely in charge of the world. We knew human beings wrote the Bible. I was taught, however, that was by divine inspiration. This meant these human words were therefore also The Word of God. 'Bible' carried weight. What God thought of my actions was a consideration for everything I did. It was like Big Brother was always watching.

I was also taught God and I were poles apart. I learned later the Christianity I was taught followed a dualistic ethic. There was a (virtual) list of Good Things: people, objects, events and emotions. There was a corresponding list of Bad versions of the same characteristics. These opposing pairings were held deep in the collective psyche. We were all unaware of how they influenced us. This is how the list might look if it were written down.

Bad	**Good**
Humankind	God
Sinful	Righteousness
Black	White
Female	Male

Body	Mind
Emotions	Logic
Private	Public
Irrationality	Rationality

There was a chasm between humans and God. There was a similar chasm between the pairs of opposites. In my young, fundamentalist world, it was either one thing or the other. Things or ideas were black or white, rational or irrational, good or bad, sinful or righteous. Talk about a 'black and white' world!

These lists were never written down or taught overtly. It was only later that I worked out they were the background to lots of commands, rules and attitudes. It might've been better if they had been written down. Then we could have seen how silly or even evil these opposites were. For example, racism and sexism thrive in a dualistic world when you look at the two lists.

Bad	**Good**
Female	Male
Black	White

I got the message. Since all humankind and I were on the 'wrong' list, I could not, without help, be close to the always-good God. The whole atonement theory was based on spanning this chasm. This was the central theme of Christianity, I was taught. It was the only framework offered for viewing myself in relation to God. I was separated by this chasm from all that was Good. That included being separated from heaven, the ultimate Good Place, and God. (Guess what Bad Place is alongside me on my side of the lists!)

Bad	**Good**
Earth	Paradise
Hell	Heaven
Me	God

I paused and hit send. What would Hope think of this? Her reply came later that evening.

Hi,

This is making a lot of sense of how life worked for our family when Dad was in his evangelical phase. I don't know what's happened to those lists for him since he's turned liberal. It is almost like evil doesn't exist for him anymore.

In haste, but keen to read more,

H

• • •

Hope,

Thanks for your reply. Here's 'more.'

In my early socialisation as a Christian, the story continued as Jesus entered this divided world. He was revered as the peacemaker, the scapegoat, the saviour.

I was told I could be 'saved' from the Bad list through Jesus' sacrifice. At his death, I was taught, he took on himself all the Badness in the world, (including mine). He was the scapegoat like I've said before. If I accepted this idea, it apparently made a difference. I was then thought good enough to be invited to God's great 'Come As You Are' party. (An irony that, as I couldn't really come-as-I-was, because the basic me was Bad!)

In some ways this seems great. Isn't it good that God bothered to send Jesus to save us from being Bad? It all carried, however, a lot of shaming and blaming. We were frequently called sinners in sermons. Later I saw we were defined as Bad by our location on the dualisms list no one talked about. But it was more deadly than that. Looking back, the idea of being Bad crept into my self-esteem. This message dulled and declared illegitimate any delight I might have had in myself. My body, and anything I might do with it, was especially suspect.

I realised all this far too late in life. The way this dualistic world operated, God, angels, heaven, good people, and salvation were all on the Good list. I was therefore on the Bad list with all the other humans in the world. With horror, I now see that I began to devalue the whole idea of being human.

Bad	Good
Me	God
Humans	Angels
Hell	Heaven
Sin & Depravity	Redemption
Sinners	The Saved

Again, I hit send, thinking though this email wasn't exceptionally long, it had some heavy concepts in it.

Hi again,

Wow. I am so glad Dad was at least a thinking evangelical. He wasn't ever stage two as your church was. I've seen what you describe in some of my cousins. They live in an isolated area. They have only one church to choose from, which is extremely basic.

How did you get out of this mindset – because you're not in it now!

Love,

H

•••

Thanks, Hope,

It was only a few years ago when I was horrified to realise that, unconsciously in my mind, being human had almost become sub-human. Growing up, I certainly knew I was not and never could be superhuman (as I was taught Jesus was.) The personal God who 'loves' you was portrayed in a way that gave me the completely opposite idea. Crazy, eh!

For me now though, there is a completely different feel when I think about the Christian myth as a journey I am taking, led by the spirit. I came to this way of thinking about the Christian life through going on spiritual retreats and talking with a spiritual director. They challenged my idea that I was not good enough.

The 'God' in this new scenario, if I think in terms of personal metaphors, is much more my friend. Yet, this 'God' is much wiser than I, so is 'someone' I see as authoritative about how I live my life.

Getting away from personal metaphors, I now think of God as a life force, or as energy. I believe 'God' is holding the universe together like dark matter and dark energy do. I believe that, even though I don't understand how God does it. But then, scientists don't understand quite how dark matter and dark energy physically work either!

Some re-enchanted people I know simply talk of God as 'Love to the nth degree.' I used to think that a wishy-washy way of looking at God. As I get more and more down this journey, however I think differently. I am more convinced of the power and energy of Love which is unconditional. In a sense, Love is all I need in my backpack as I walk this Way. It is also the air which surrounds me. It is the energy which courses right through me.

Each day the journey stretches before me. If I can, I embrace it and walk it. The best image of this I've found is David Griebner's parable, '*The Carpenter and the Unbuilder.*' Briefly, the story goes like this. You need to get it and read the whole story for yourself. There are lovely passages in it.

A Carpenter receives an invitation to dinner with the ruler of the land. He sets off but is unsure of the way. He gets 'stuck' in a house he builds around himself and lives in for a while. He then moves on and gets 'stuck' again. One day, a stranger comes along. He helps the carpenter (metaphorically) 'unbuild' the shelter he has built. (The shelter was originally meant only for one night, but the safety and security of it 'captured' the Carpenter and he always stops travelling when he builds a house.) The 'Unbuilder' finally persuades the Carpenter to continue the journey. There is a moving passage describing what they do the next morning:

> Silently they sat through the morning in the carpenter's front yard. Slowly it began to seem as though they were already on the journey. As that feeling grew and grew, it suddenly didn't seem like any decision needed to be made; it just happened. With a deep sense of freedom, they were off.[41]

Griebner writes that was the pattern most days. First waiting, then the 'sense of journeying wrapped itself around even their waiting.' That meant they could resume the journey without anxiety. He writes, 'in the stillness of their hearts they made room for the path and the path seemed to come to them.'

Just like the Carpenter, I encounter various experiences. I rely on the spirit's resources and spirit-filled people like the Unbuilder to help meet those experiences. I know as I journey, (as I always say at the end of a service): "Love surrounds me every moment of every day."

I fail some of the challenges in front of me. Other times, I succeed. Climbing some hills on the way is exhausting. There are pits of despair that can last for days or weeks. But occasionally, I get a view of where I've been and where I am now. Then I know I've made progress since last time I looked.

Paying attention to the leading of the spirit is a learned skill. Following the direction of myth is hard. But, when I do that, I know I am becoming better acquainted with my own Self. I do not feel like a depraved sinner. I feel loved and accepted. I can do what I can do. When I can't, the spirit and other spirit-led people are there to help. Caroline Myss describes her journey as if everything around her is the

Divine. That means for her, she is always in God. Though she isn't on the kind of plane which means that she can see it, she believes she is always 'in the light.' Surrounded this way, it follows for her then, that if she asks for help, she can trust that everything in the creation will be helping her.[42]

Walking this journey, I know am on the way to becoming the human I am meant to be. As I take this route to becoming more human, as John Spong said, I know I am approaching the divine. It really is right, that saying, "the truth will set you free." The truth – metaphorical and mythical truth – has set me free.

Hope, it's such a gift to talk with you. Writing this down has been helpful for me. I hope some of it helps with your own pathfinding.

Let me know when you want to meet again.

Your friend and minister.

8 — Being in church as a re-enchanted person

Hope emailed in reply. She'd loved the metaphor of the Carpenter story and accessed it online. She'd started reading it each morning as preparation for the day.

What a great idea, I mused. I wished I'd thought of doing that myself. It would be a better way of starting the day than listening to the news. That contemporary parable always gets me into the right frame of mind. A mindset that is more alert to spiritual and mystical metaphors around me in the ordinary world.

We arranged to meet at *The Cup* on Thursday after the bookshop closed for the day. Hope wanted to discuss how to survive being part of her conventional church, while she transitions from disenchantment to re-enchantment. She thought we might need more than just a lunch hour.

Hope repeated her question on Thursday. Flat whites sat in front of us. We had one of *The Cup's* famous double cheese rolls each.

"Where does the conventional faith fit now for me? I'm on this other journey that hardly gets mentioned in a stage three church."

"One writer who might help here is Marcus Borg," I replied.

"The guy who wrote *Putting Away Childish Things*?" Hope asked. "I've ordered it, but it hasn't arrived yet."

"Yes, that's the one. Borg distinguishes between believing and 'beloving.' He says what people meant by 'believing' in pre-Enlightenment thinking, was more like 'beloving.' He describes beloving as a trusting, loving attitude. It is not a head-based belief in precise formulas or creeds. The idea of faith then, he argues, was more like the idea of trusting someone or a path. This is different from a faith which depends on believing in church-approved propositions."

Hope was nodding as I spoke. "I was reading about the heaps of words we have now in church. The article said all those confessions and creeds are products of the Reformation and Enlightenment?"

"Well, what would have been important in splitting from the mothership, the Catholic church? It was vital to clearly set down your beliefs which differed from pre-existing catholic faith. Many confessions were written during the Reformation. They weren't confessing sin. They were 'confessing the faith' or bearing witness to the faith. Those two expressions mean the same thing. Those protesting Protestants were stating in black and white what seemed to them to be right and true," I said.

"What were the most important confessions for Presbyterians?" asked Hope.

"First, there was the original Scots' Confession written in 1560. That was the year the Scottish protestant church was officially formed by the Scottish parliament."

"There was also a Heidelberg Confession written in 1563 which was widely used after 1619."

"The Westminster Confession was written in 1647 in a later stage of British Protestantism. Calvinism was at its height, which you can tell from the text."

"Did any other church have confessions?" asked Hope.

"The Anglican church in England had what they called the 39 Articles. They were written in 1563. They were called Articles, but they were essentially a confession of faith too."

"Were confessions only written around the time of the Reformation?" asked Hope.

"Much later during World War II, in defiance of Hitler, a group formed in opposition to the state-endorsed Lutheran church. They called themselves The Confessing Church. That group, which contained Karl Barth and Dietrich Bonhoeffer, wrote the Barmen Confession. It had a different form from the others. It directly contradicted the assumptions underlying Hitler's power. It was a brave document to write, given the time. They were all brave documents, I guess. They were all written under contentious circumstances."

"They were in danger of losing their lives for the cause in chaotic times. They would want to know exactly what they believed and why," commented Hope thoughtfully.

"Later in the 18th century, when codifying of belief and setting out of propositions happened, that suited the Enlightenment mindset, I said."

"If there is a clear statement of belief, then people could be taught it. Some confessions have a question-and-answer version for teaching to children and young people. They're called catechisms. They were taught and learned by rote. Some older people still going to church now, grew up learning the catechism. They all seem to remember the first question and answer of the Westminster Catechism: 'Q: What is man's chief end? A: To enjoy and glorify God forever.'"

"Funny they included enjoying God. Wasn't God made out to be a bit of a tyrant at the time?" joked Hope, irony in her voice.

"I think they came to think that too as they got older!" I said.

"Borg talks about something different from believing a whole lot of written confessional stuff?" asked Hope.

"Yes, Borg's approach revolves around a more loving trusting relationship. It might be with Jesus, or with 'God.' It could be a trusting relationship with the spirit as we're led through the journey. It could be the feeling of being loved we get when we're centred and grounded and on the way."

"So how does knowing all this background help with coping in a conventional church?" asked Hope.

"It's good to go to church in a 'beloving' mode of being. A church service might rely heavily on words and ideas and beliefs. You can, however, allow yourself to … I don't know … kind of float through it," I said.

"You could think of moving through the service as if you were steering a boat along the underground aquifer. Or you could think of it as paddling a kayak for an hour on the ocean of Love which is God."

"During the service, keep alert for those moments we've talked about. Those times when there's some connectedness. Look for the 'I-Thou' forming. Enjoy those moments, even if it means letting the next few minutes of church pass you by. That reminds me of a quote (often wrongly attributed to George Eliot):

> Oh, the comfort – the inexpressible comfort of feeling safe with a person, having neither to weigh thoughts, nor measure words, but pouring them all out, just as they are, chaff and grain together; knowing that a faithful hand will take and sift them – keep what is worth keeping – and with the breath of kindness blow the rest away.[43]

"I like that. On the journey, that's what any genuine helper will do with anything you confide in them. You can do that with church if you are in an open accepting, seeking frame of mind. You keep what is worth keeping. You blow the rest away with a 'breath of kindness.' On the other hand, if you go to church feeling angry, you'll find everything is chaff!"

Hope laughed. "And haven't I been in that position a lot recently," she said. "Though I've been calmer in church since you and I have been talking about journeying and stuff."

"As you read more, formerly irritating things are easier to absorb when you get the mythical meaning underneath them. Some of my questioning friends got very uptight about the Trinity, for example. It was as if they had been beaten about the head with it when they were younger. Later, they found the doctrine of the Trinity was formed a long time after the biblical books were written. They saw it as fake and were annoyed because they felt they'd been conned," I said.

"I have to say the Trinity is still a bit of a mystery to me," said Hope ruefully.

"There was a word I learned in ministry training. It left me a lot more kindly disposed towards the Trinity. It's a neat Greek word *perichoresis – peri* = around, *choresis* from the same root word as choreography. The lecturer told us Trinity was a model of community. Using perichoresis to describe it was saying the three 'persons' of the Trinity danced around together, intertwined and intertwining."

"That's a cool image!" said Hope. "Kind of like what we do at square dancing. Only it's not square, since there are only three of them."

"Well, one of the feminist objections to the Trinity is that it is 'two men and a bird.' But, why not add Wisdom to the Trinity and make it a Quaternary? Then you have two 'male' persons and two 'female' persons, the spirit and Wisdom. So, there you have your square!" We both chuckled in delight. Playing around with metaphors always lightened up the conversation.

"It's an evocative idea, the Trinity (or Quaternary) dancing around. At times you catch more of a glimpse of one person than the others. I've had occasions when the God 'person' was more important. Other days Jesus is centre stage for me. At times, the spirit is all important.

Wisdom features often too in my life. Not always my wisdom, sadly!"

Hope broke in. "A friend who's in rural ministry told me she reckoned farmers related more to God. They felt nearer to the Creator than Jesus or the spirit. That made sense since farmers interact heaps with the environment and nature. They keep glimpsing the 'God as creator' figure most in their work."

"Interesting. I wonder whether artists relate more to spirit, especially, say musicians? Particularly flute players, perhaps. Their medium is the breath. You could think about that when you're next playing the flute," I suggested.

"I'll try!" Hope laughed. "That's an idea, coming into conventional church relaxed and in journey-mode. I might then have a quiet enough spirit to float. Or I would have a free enough mind to reinterpret or translate what is going on. I don't know if I could do that very well in a stage two church. Say, something like the charismatic one my sister attends. It might be possible in a stage three congregation, though."

"Sadly, it might be that you need to reduce church attendance. Or, to save your journey you may need to leave altogether, temporarily, or permanently. That's if the dissonance gets too much. It's vital you don't let conventional church become a shelter of avoidance like the carpenter's shelters he built along the way. It's important your personal journey continues to be the most significant thing. Remember, it doesn't mean you're giving up the Christian journey. It means you're walking another route in the same beloving faith-path."

"I suspect people in the church will misunderstand that," said Hope ruefully. "Though, people like my Dad would understand some of it."

"Growing up in the Christian church, we are taught not to upset or offend people. We've been told that's the kind thing to do. I wouldn't advocate going around deliberately and unnecessarily upsetting people. But you do need to keep on growing as your own person. You are the only one who will make that a priority for yourself," I said.

"It might be that you talk about other things with your stage three friends. It might be that you answer questions but don't push them to change their minds before they are ready. Or you can gently suggest a book you think they would cope with and see how it goes. You wouldn't have liked being pushed yourself. Expecting people to suddenly be where you are isn't fair. On the other hand, you might find they are longing to move on. They may not know how to tell you, or their church, they want something different. I've been surprised by the interest people show when I thought they wouldn't," I said.

"Jesus spoke straight from the shoulder at times, didn't he?" asked Hope. "I remember him pushing back hard at the Pharisees. He didn't agree with the men intending to stone that woman. He even disagreed with his own mother!"

"Good point. You know that story when his mother and siblings ask for him? His family wanted him to come home and stop working out his call. We need to steel ourselves to not let even our family pull us back. It's not the conventional 'Christian' way, resisting kind, well-meaning advice. But you're not in conventional Christian territory anymore. You are in stage four, looking to find stage five."

"Maybe it's about balance," mused Hope. "If you've been around a lot of stage three people, seek out some stage four friends. Or, read a book that's more journey-friendly, as a kind of antidote!"

We laughed together at the image.

Perhaps we laughed because if we hadn't, we'd have cried. I knew it was one of the hardest things in my life when I found the church I served and had loved didn't satisfy my quest for my Self anymore. I felt more and more like a fish out of water in conventional church settings. I was fortunate in my present position, where leeway was allowed. And I wasn't responsible for leading all our services. Still, collegial ministers' association meetings and the occasional funeral are hard to negotiate. Hope, in all her newness to the journey, had just given me a good piece of advice which I could do well to follow. I told her so and she flushed with pleasure.

"Happy to help," she said with a mock bow.

"Hey, just before we move on, let me tell you about one guy who's bravely and publicly changed his direction. David Gushee's an American academic. Though he was a Baptist ethics professor, he's changed his mind on the issue of acceptability of gays in the church. His sister came out to their family, and he had to rethink his position."[44]

"He went public with his new views. He apologised to any gay people he'd hurt with his previous rejection. I heard him speak in

New Zealand. He got a lot of flak from evangelicals. Since then, he's published two more books. They show he's rejecting hard-line, American-style evangelical positions.[45] I got his last book the other day, and was struck by something Brian McLaren wrote in the Foreword.

> I've had the honour of reading and endorsing several of David's books, so I've had a front row seat in watching his transformation and migration. Step-by-step he has made clear what he needed to leave, and in this book he makes it equally clear that instead of moving from one static location to another, he has moved from a static location to a dynamic peregrination, from a place to a path, from "Here I stand" to "Here is the path I am now following."[46]

"That really sums up what you've been saying, doesn't it?" asked Hope. "What I am questioning is the stay-in-one-place kind of Christianity. I am querying the attitude that tempts you, once you find a safe place, to stay there. The new approach we've been talking about is a moving thing, an exploring, discovering, journey."

"What's more," I add, "that 'here I stand' statement is attributed to Martin Luther. Way back in 1517 he stated his different theology and stood by it. The new protestant church which followed did the same. They staked out a definite position which they laid alongside the Catholic position. Some people in both churches keep on journeying. Many haven't though. They've stayed standing still, in the same place."

"From 'Here I stand' to 'Here is the path I am now following' is a great metaphor. That's the change you're experiencing right now. Of course, friends and family and the conventional church might prefer you to stay in one place. They'd rather you don't walk on from where you are now. Your changes unsettle them as well as unsettling you," I said.

"Remember what you preached in church the other day?" Hope reminded me, "'Without a vision the people perish.' Perhaps it should be 'Without a path your faith perishes.'"

"Like if you stop walking in your physical life, your muscles waste away," I added. "If you don't exercise your spiritual muscles by walking the path, your strength goes," I suggested.

"I like that," said Hope with satisfaction. "What are the details of Gushee's book? I wonder whether I would dare give it to Dad. I'd need to read it first."

She scribbled the details on a nearby napkin, then stuffed it into her backpack. Telling me she would see me next week, she left me to my thoughts.

9 — Where do the sacraments fit now?

"After the baptismal service last Sunday, I've been wondering," said Hope as we settled down with our coffees the following week. "How do Christian church rituals fit with the new journey we've been talking about? You described them as being part of the 'clothing' which the church thought was needed to make the spirit visible."

"Do we need rituals anymore? That is, if you're walking a journey where spirit is visible to you pretty much all the time? Particularly, do we need church rituals? I'm thinking quite differently about God and the Christian narrative. Do conventional rituals hang together anymore?" she asked.

"Let's start with baptism," I replied. "In our denomination, that's the first ritual a person engages in, as a baby. Your parents had you baptised as a baby, right?"

"Yes. I have a baptismal certificate at home. I was about 6 months old. My grandfather baptised me. He was a minister too."

"OK. I was baptised too. I was 13 years old when I decided to ask for baptism. It was full immersion in front of a full church. I came up out of the water looking like a baby seal, wet hair, clothes, and all. Major embarrassment! That's how Baptists do it."

"I'm glad I was six months old," Hope laughed. "If the water did trickle down my forehead, I can't remember being embarrassed. Why the two types of baptism?"

"As you said, the sacraments, including baptism, are some of those pieces of 'clothing.' They've been draped over the fountain of the spirit to make the spirit more visible. I find it interesting that in baptism water is chosen as the sign of the spirit. There's a connection right there to that aquifer/fountain metaphor."

"Huh! Everything is connected in the end," said Hope.

"Seems so. Baptism is the entry point to officially belonging to the church. There are two views on how you enter. One is that a child is brought in by their parents when they are young. Like you were. There's a First Testament promise used to support that. It's a promise, apparently from God, for you and your children and your children's children."[47]

"The other view is that you join the church later. The timing is when you as an individual have decided that's what you want and what you believe in. It's called believer's baptism. It's usually left to what's called the 'age of discretion.' That's when church leaders think you're old enough to make up your own mind."

"13 is still pretty young to be making a lifelong commitment to a religion," commented Hope.

"I agree. I didn't become a church member till two years later in a separate act. 15 is still young for that, I think. Opinion varied then in my local church as to whether baptism and membership should go together."

"The older adult members were nervous about younger members. My church's constitution back then had a clause that under 18-year-olds couldn't vote in church meetings. I asked why? It was so young members couldn't sell out the church buildings out from under the older generation. There were never enough of us under-18-year-olds to do anything so radical!"

We laughed together.

"It was common for older members to distrust the ideas of the younger, fearing they would be too iconoclastic," I said.

"How far back does baptism go as entry to the church?" asked Hope.

"In the Early Church, adults joining the movement were baptised. Our official church creeds evolved from the baptismal formulas candidates agreed to so they could be baptised. The formulas covered basic beliefs; Jesus as son of God, the Holy Spirit, God as creator, Jesus' life and death and resurrection…."

"This took a lot of courage at first. Before the emperor Constantine, in 312 CE, declared that Christianity was allowed to be practised in the Roman Empire, it was a subversive statement to say, 'Jesus is Lord.' Until then, only the emperor was considered divine. The expected statement in the Roman Empire was 'Caesar is Lord.' To put another person in Caesar's place would have been treason. That's why claiming Jesus as Lord, as part of a faith statement which qualified you for baptism, was a dangerous act. They were a brave group, those early Christians. They paid for their courage with their lives in many cases."

We both nodded silently. The brief space of quiet felt like an in memoriam for those brave women and men.

I continued.

"You know the Nicene and Apostles' creeds? They were put together years later from different formulas. The formulas were used for baptism in different pockets of the growing early church movement: Antioch, Jerusalem, Rome…"

"Yeah, I know that stuff. We 'did' the Early Church Councils in Theology 101," said Hope. "Constantine called them together, didn't he, to get uniformity throughout the empire."

"Yes. That underlines what I was going to say. Baptism developed as a means of knowing who was 'in.' Therefore, not being baptised defined who was 'out.' That's what happens when you start any kind of group. As soon as you declare what makes an insider, you are also declaring who isn't," I said.

"So how does infant baptism work if the baby doesn't know what is going on?" asked Hope.

"Remember, I was raised Baptist. I see infant baptism as a public commitment by the parents to raise their child in the faith. It's a little like Mary and Joseph bringing Jesus to the temple not long after he was born. I see the weight of promises made at a child's baptism as being on the parents. They declare their faith. They promise to bring up the child in the faith," I said.

"I get the impression infant baptism was how adults, baptised by immersion as they entered the new, early church movement, ensured their families were part of that movement right from birth."

"The adults were following Jesus being baptised in the Jordan by John. Their children though, had a different kind of baptism, still based on water symbolism?" asked Hope.

"I guess my view is a little biased because of my Baptist up bringing. I think the symbolism of the water in infant baptism is a little weak. Eastern Orthodox churches dunk the naked baby three times into the water. They really go for it! I found this amazing picture of a Greek Orthodox baptism. The priest was holding up a dripping wet, naked, bouncing baby boy. The baby was screaming his lungs out! Must make baptismal services interesting!" I replied. Hope chuckled.

"Are infant baptisms in the western church only by sprinkling water on the baby's forehead?" asked Hope.

"Usually. It's tidier!" I smiled. "But when I was just starting out as a minister, I asked advice of an older minister. He said I could sprinkle the baby with water as you were. Or, he said, I could pour a jug of water over the child. Or, I could immerse them completely. I did that last one once, but that's a long story," I said.

"Tell me about your baptism and Baptist theology about believer's baptism," enquired Hope.

"I've always felt being immersed in water in front of a whole congregation takes a lot of courage. You don't look great coming up out of the water. As I said before, you look like a baby seal. It was a big deal, especially for a teenage girl. You needed to be convinced you wanted this step. Looking back, I remember a genuine feeling of 'a call' to this next step of discipleship. Of course, there was always a lot of emotion around the services where they asked people to commit," I said.

"Our contemporary baptism by immersion springs from the Reformation, actually. A key motive in reforming movements then was a desire to return to Christianity's 'true' roots. Much of what reformers thought of as 'add-ons' were stripped away."

"Like indulgences and saints and feasts days?" asked Hope.

"That's right. Immersion baptism reached back to Jesus' baptism in the Jordan by his cousin John. You know, John the Baptist. I have no doubt Jesus was spiritually involved in it. You could also think of it as being like the launches and photo ops used now to celebrate and promote new ventures. That moment marked Jesus' transition from carpenter to itinerant rabbi. (Or perhaps it was the Gospel writers who later saw that moment from that perspective)," I suggested.

"In the same way, believer's baptism was taught to us as a visible sign of the inner transition from being a sinner to being saved. We were taught that it was like Jesus dying, going down into the tomb, and being raised again. We were seen as dying to our old life and being raised in Christ. There's a passage in the Second Testament which says:

We were therefore buried with him through baptism into death in order that, just as Christ was raised from the dead through the glory of the Father, we too may live a new life."[48]

"That is a stronger symbolism than infant baptism," commented Hope. "It fits the idea of water being used better, too. When did the two ways of doing baptism start – do only Baptists do believer's baptism?" she asked.

"The prevailing catholic system, pre-Reformation, was infant baptism. The new Lutheran church and other churches influenced by John Calvin, which were the beginnings of Presbyterianism, carried on with infant baptism," I replied.

"As the Reformation progressed, the Anabaptist branch of the church broke away from the Lutheran branch and the Calvin-led Presbyterian way. Anabaptists adopted believer's baptism and made other radical changes. Anabaptist was a name given by others to this radical approach. It means twice-baptisers. Of course, Anabaptist churches don't think they are baptising people twice, as they don't recognise infant baptism."

"It's interesting that Lutherans found this shocking. I get the impression that Lutherans hadn't really intended to change the church completely, just to modernise a few ideas and practices. Making significant changes to sacraments like baptism was a step too far. Distinct branches of different denominations began to develop after Luther's one act of defiance. I suppose once there's one protest, it makes it more possible for others to protest too," I said.

"Did the Anabaptist movement produce the Baptist church here in our country?" asked Hope.

"The Anabaptist movement in continental Europe evolved to produce groups like the Mennonites, who later emigrated to America."

"The New Zealand Baptist church came from English roots. The English Baptist movement was influenced by Anabaptist ideas, but they were more a reformed breakaway from Anglicanism. They distanced themselves from the Anabaptist movement in the 17th century. John Smyth, a founding minister of the English Baptist Church, went from being Anglican to Puritan, then English Separatist[49] to Baptist Separatist."

Hope nodded thoughtfully, "that sounds like a tricky journey from what I know of that period in English history. That was when the monarchy was attacked and later restored wasn't it! Civil war was raging throughout the country."

"Brave people stood up for their principles on both sides. Infant baptism's been a contentious issue in the church for a long time. My fellow Baptists looked down on infant baptism as it wasn't the child making their own decision. Now I see it as a teachable and pivotal moment for parents. They can renew their own faith commitment when they promise to raise their child in the faith," I said.

"My main problem as a Presbyterian minister came when people who didn't come to church at all, suddenly arrived with their new child and asked me to conduct a baptism at home. Baptism is essentially an entry into the Christian community. I believe it needs to happen within that community. Those parents were quite clear that they didn't see why getting their child 'christened,' as they called it, should have any implied connection for them of becoming regular members of a church."

"What did you do in those cases?" asked Hope.

"I offered a baby naming ceremony or a blessing. We were generally able to make it a special occasion which celebrated their child and their family. The arrival of a new child is a special time for a family. I admired those parents. They loved their new baby and were determined to celebrate their child's arrival with a spiritual ceremony. Why coming to church didn't suit them was sometimes part of the conversation and sometimes not."

"I love the way baptism happens at our church," said Hope. "It's always such a community occasion. I noticed last Sunday that the congregation makes promises to the family too. The family obviously appreciated it. I love it when older siblings light the candle and pour the water into the font."

"It just goes to show. A ritual may not 'fit' official theology at all points, but if it's carried out with sincerity, commitment, and love, it can still connect us to the spirit working in our lives. This is where the journeying metaphor links in with organised religious ritual. Both infant baptism and believer's baptism can act as first steps, or at least important steps, on the journey to our true Selves," I said.

"I see believer's baptism as showing everyone 'where you're at' as an adult. Is confirmation the same?" asked Hope.

"Confirmation is the companion ritual to infant baptism. The name gives you the idea. In confirmation, the person baptised as a baby gets to 'confirm' their choice to remain on the path as an adult. In contrast to the drama and riskiness of believer's baptism, I find most confirmation ceremonies tame. They can be as simple as standing up front answering some questions, and that's it. Though I suppose for some people standing up at the front of the church, with everyone's attention on you, is risky enough!"

"Recently, I've asked people to write their own versions of the creed using a four part structure: 'I believe in God… Jesus… Spirit… Church….' I get them to pick a theme which engages them in their real life. Then they write what they believe about those four concepts in the light of their theme. That makes their faith statement a key part of their confirmation."

"Huh, how did that turn out?" asked Hope.

"Great! Two teenage siblings chose basketball (which they were fanatical about) for their theme. For them, God was the designer of the game and maker of the rules. Jesus was playing on the team alongside them. For them, the Spirit was the team doctor. The church was cheering them on, as their home crowd. It was cool. Anyone could see from the roles they assigned that they really understood deep down what it was all about."

"Mmmm. I wonder what theme I would choose," mused Hope. "Music? Books? Tramping?" she continued. "My cousin who's Catholic did a whole confirmation thing when he was eleven. They did it at school, with most of their class joining in. I think it was called…"

"First Communion?" I offered.

"That's it. They all wore white and some of the girls wore veils," said Hope.

"White represents purity," I continued. "The veils aren't wedding imagery. Women used to have their heads covered in church. It's a vestigial remnant of that. Head covering is taken to represent humility before God, modesty, and reverence."

"I notice the boys don't have to wear veils! You wouldn't call most eleven-year-old boys 'humble, modest and reverent,'" said Hope.

"Good point," I replied. "Some gender inequality there. Girls don't have to wear veils at First Communion anymore. They usually wear something in their hair as a nod towards that tradition."

"The connection between communion and confirmation has faded in our denomination. That's because we've opened up communion to children and adults who haven't been baptised. Earlier you didn't take communion before you were confirmed, or in Baptist churches until you were baptised. Then the person became a communicant member. That is, someone admitted to communion. That might be why, where children take communion, confirmation's become less of a big deal. It's actually still really important as a commitment, though," I said.

"Confirmation then, is a deeper commitment to the church?" asked Hope. "That seems like a funny thing for young people to do. Like me, they might be questioning the church. Isn't this the time they are most likely to be disenchanted by it?" Her face was honestly puzzled and enquiring.

"Exactly. It does seem like a contradiction. That will partly account for the vastly reduced number of confirmations compared with when I was a teenager."

"People who are disenchanted with church, yet still wanting to be confirmed, could however, see Confirmation as confirming their new quest. The church brings you this far on your journey. The journey doesn't just start now with this new perspective. It's been ongoing since birth. Baptism as a baby signals that, for the child and their family. They are saying that, for them, the Christian church is the backdrop for their spiritual path, not an Islamic mosque or Jewish synagogue."

"Your journey isn't just *starting* at confirmation but *continuing* in a new format. Confirmation can say to others watching that there is a journey and you've been on it and still intend to walk it. Even though the terrain has changed a lot, that might be a good way to look at the ritual of confirmation. What do you think?" I asked.

"Yeah, sounds like there's mileage in that – excuse the pun. When do confirmations happen?" asked Hope.

"I like doing them on a communion Sunday. Any first Sunday of the month would work in our church. Some denominations do confirmations in a big group on Easter. People often have their parents present. That can lead to some negotiation on dates if their family lives elsewhere. Writing the personal creed takes some time."

"Mmmm. Can you send me a copy of what those teenagers did with the basketball motif? I'd better go now. I'm meeting Charlie for a burger," said Hope.

I noted this with an inner smile. Hope didn't realise how often Charlie's name had come up in our conversations over the last few weeks, and not only after the *Lord of the Rings* binge marathon.

All I said out loud was, "Go well."

10 — Communicating about Communion

The next day my text notification pinged.

> H: We didn't discuss communion

> Me: Was thinking that.

> H: What's with communion? It's creepy. Words about blood with red grape juice or wine! Eew!

> Me: Symbols remember, not reality.

> H: Is Jesus' blood really the wine like the words say?

> Me: No, goes back further to the Exodus.

> Me: This will take explaining! Might change to email.

> Me: BTW read Ex 11 & 12 b4 u read email.

This was an opportunity to show Hope how myths had a long life. Also, that they morphed to suit a new generation or to adapt to a twist in the journey.

> Hi Hope

> I've attached some creeds I wrote as a broader kind of 'creed' people could say in church without telling lies about what they believed or didn't believe. I wrote quite a few new affirmations in my former church too. (See Appendix 1)

> Communion. Hmmm. Quite a history, not just political history now between denominations, but it goes way back further than many people think.

> I hope you read those chapters in Exodus. You probably heard in Sunday school about the cute baby Moses in the bulrushes rescued by an Egyptian princess. The stuff fairy tales are made of… and that's a clue.

> Scholars think that this great legend of the Exodus was written up and expanded hundreds of years later when the Jews were more settled. When the tumult has died, the histories get written. Often, they're written to a theme in the historian's head. Happens today too.

> Exodus became a Big Myth for the Jewish people. It highlighted their deliverance (by God, as they wrote the story) out of slavery in Egypt.

They'd fled there, remember, years before during famine in the time of Joseph-of-the-many-coloured-coat fame.[50]

Centuries later, Moses, his brother Aaron and his sister Miriam were key leaders in the movement out of Egypt. The story goes that they led the people to what they called The Promised Land. Of course, now we know there were legitimate residents there already. We're putting up with the ramifications of that occupation even today.

The key connection between communion and the Exodus is the final meal on the last night of bondage. They were instructed to make unleavened bread because there was not enough time to let the bread rise. They were to kill a lamb and smear the blood of the lamb on the lintel and doorposts of their houses.

The final plague was that the Angel of Death would pass over the city and kill every firstborn in a house not protected by blood. This sounds barbaric to our post-Enlightenment ears. Remember, this is an embellished story. Symbols have been added to make the story larger than life. Also remember the concept of blood sacrifices saving people from a bad fate was well known in those times. This would also make sense to Jewish people in Jesus' time.

The marking of the doorposts was like us needing to have an invisible watermark in our passports. That shows we are citizens of a country and therefore allowed to pass into another country. Or it would be like those stamps they give you at night clubs. If you have a pass-out, you don't have to pay again when you return. (Fortunately, no lambs are harmed in either of those contemporary processes!)

Notice the key elements were blood and bread.

There's one clue this story was written later, after there had been time to reflect on this hasty evacuation. That is the ultra-clear instructions God apparently gave the leaders about celebrating Passover. They read like a well discussed, carefully constructed prayer book.

Passover is still a yearly festival within the Jewish religion today. In his narrative, Jesus is placed in Jerusalem at the time of the Passover leading up to his crucifixion. Celebrating Passover in Jerusalem was a great occasion. Jerusalem had heaps of extra visitors, like holiday places here have an influx of tourists in summertime.

The later Passover meals in Jesus' time and now, (the name comes from the Angel 'passing over' the marked houses) did not necessarily use a lamb. The wine served at Passover symbolically substituted for the blood of the lamb and unleavened bread is used.[51]

It's not truly clear if the last supper Jesus had with his disciples was a Passover meal. Usually, Passover was held in a home and children took part in the ritual. The disciples would have been fortunate if someone had given them an upper room in their house to celebrate the feast with Jerusalem probably totally booked out.

Whatever the reality, at what we now call the Last Supper there seems to have been bread and wine. The symbolism of the two elements was then attached to Jesus' shed blood and Jesus' broken body by the words which were, we are told, said by Jesus. I personally think this association might have been made later by the disciples as they tried to work out what was happening after Jesus' death.[52]

In protestant churches from the radical reformation onwards, communion is thought of as more of a meal of remembrance, not a re-enactment. The elements are regarded as ordinary bread and wine which stand as symbols.

In a church with a more formal view, the bread and wine, once consecrated, are regarded as very holy indeed. That has consequences about who is allowed to serve and celebrate communion or mass. It also affects how leftover elements are treated. We can talk about that another time if you are interested.

There's no getting round it. Crucifixion was a terrible way to die. It's one of the worst methods of killing humankind has invented. In Jesus' case, the violence is worse because he seems to have been innocent of the charges laid against him. Whoever was being crucified, it was a bloody mess.

I joke to children at church that if they were repeating exactly a farewell meal I might have had with them, they'd be drinking hot chocolate and eating pavlova, but that's not quite right. The disciples were eating a Passover meal with Jesus. There would not have been party foods on the table. It was more significant than that.

So, communion wine links through Jesus and the Last Supper with the blood of the lamb at the original 'passing over' in Egypt. This would not have worried Jewish people of the time who understood blood sacrifice. It was their belief that blood needed to be shed to take away wrong. This happened all the time in the temple in Jesus' day. They were used to the 'blood and guts' of sacrificial ritual. The Temple in Jerusalem was designed for it. Have a look at some pictures of the temple layout and you'll see.

On the surface it is not familiar to us, especially sacrifice of animals.

But the concept of sacrifice on behalf of others is familiar in our time. We've picked up the symbolism of spilt blood representing sacrifice. We use red poppies on Anzac Day to commemorate blood spilt. Blood shed by dying soldiers is linked in a myth-like way to red poppies growing in Flanders' fields where they fought in World War I.

Both drink and food are life giving. We can acknowledge that without needing to refer to blood, if that's a real problem for contemporary congregations. I usually refer to the cup of wine at communion as a Cup of Blessing. I call the bread the Bread of Life.

We're also used to food in other rituals. In our wider culture we use food as a symbol of coming together. Wedding cake's a good example. In America, the bride and groom feed each other the first slice. The wedding 'breakfast' is called that because it's seen as the first meal in a couple's new life. Others are invited to eat with them to celebrate bringing two families together.

In New Zealand Māori culture after the speeches and the hongi of greeting (touching of noses), food is shared. This is seen as mingling the manuhiri (visitors) and the tangata whenua (people of the place) together as one group. It serves to bring the formerly separate into ordinary life together (from tapu to noa).

So we 21st century people do know about blood being a symbol of extreme giving. We are familiar with eating together as a symbol of being brought together. Some liturgies we've used in church use new associations. I've attached one. (See Appendix 3) I wish I'd been brave enough to write more.

I remember years ago a student asking why we didn't ever have communion using beer and pies. I thought that intriguing. At the time it was a little risqué for me! Later, when we wrapped up a Sunday evening chapel series that student attended, I did use unconventional elements, which we had discussed together beforehand. We decided a Moro chocolate bar and a Red Bull drink could be used as communion elements with a theme of the energy they provided.[53] We got the giggles when I served myself the Moro bar. It almost stuck my teeth together! Silence fell for a long minute. The theme of energy and the spirit giving us wings won through, however.

I've often thought communion happens whenever two or more people eat and drink together. Communion is when we pay attention to each other. In this sense, our coffee shop conversations could be regarded as communion.

As often happens in organised churches, communion can take on an aura of holiness and magic. Then it can bear little resemblance to the blunt, open honesty of hastily eaten food in that Egyptian slave ghetto or that curiously sad meal in that upper room.

What was it exactly that Jesus might want us to 'do in remembrance of him?' Whatever we do to remember him, it needs to be authentic.

I have gone on, haven't I? One story to finish.

I was thrilled to join a congregation of the Church of the Saviour in Washington DC on a Sunday in 2013. It ended with communion. We lined up in the aisle between chairs placed in rows in The Potter's House, their 60+ year old coffee shop ministry. I wasn't really noticing the people around me in the line. I did know the young woman in front of me was there for the first time. We'd talked earlier.

The wine was in a pottery chalice and the unleavened bread on a flat pottery plate. Suddenly, I roused from my dreamy state to find the young woman in front of me turning to offer me the elements. I was staggered. I thought, "What a way to include someone first time up; bring them right into the heart of the most important sacrament of the community."

Then I realised I was to serve the person behind me. I grinned to myself. No one in the room except my husband knew I was ordained. Yet, they were trusting me, trusting each of us, with serving this special meal to each other. There was a beautiful freedom and generosity about this custom. It didn't matter whether they'd been there for 60 years or 60 minutes. Very different from the protocol in a heavily liturgical church.

Our church has rules about only special (ordained) people being allowed to celebrate and serve and say certain words. Yet at the Last Supper the man who would betray Jesus was eating from the same dish as his victim. True inclusion brought vulnerability and risk then. It still does now.

That's a lot for an email. Let me know when you've digested it and whether you have questions. We can meet again whenever you're ready. Go well.

f & m

11 — Myth in scripture and our daily lives.

Next morning my inbox had a reply from Hope. She said she'd found my email on communion helpful. It was making her think about her own attitudes to who was 'in' and who was 'out.' She wondered if there were any ways groups could form without implicitly excluding others. She added:

> I'm reconsidering what was vilified in my former church as doubt and backsliding. I see now it was only sometimes about people getting lazy or tired of the self-discipline involved in being Christian. I now think that most of the time it was people moving into stage four but not being able to discuss it with others.
>
> Just looked at Brian McLaren's website. He's just published 'Faith After Doubt: Why Your Beliefs Stopped Working and what to do about it.' I got a Kindle version. As far as I've been able to skim already, it seems he's covering the same ground we've been dealing with in our discussions. He recommends an amazing list of authors; all ones you've talked of and more.
>
> That made me wonder whether this is not just a few individuals questioning their faith. Is it also a culture-wide (Western culture at least) movement of questioning and searching? That fits what you said about Phyllis Tickle saying this sorting out is a thing Christianity does about every half millennium. Didn't she quote someone saying it was like a 500-year rummage sale?[54]
>
> That fits what I'm doing exactly. I feel like I'm sorting through all my religious clutter. I'm deciding what to keep. I'm choosing what to pass off to the rummage sale. I'm glad I started asking questions now. These days there's a substantial literature for resource and support. It must have been harder when you started your stage four.
>
> Can we meet on Thursday after work? Same place different time?
>
> H

I was struck by Hope's comments. When I began to question orthodox faith 15 to 20 years ago, there were only a few people who were speaking up. Dave Tomlinson's *Post Evangelical* came out in 1995, just as I began ministry training. Then there was the alt worship movement, which I discovered in the early 2000s in New Zealand with Mike Riddell, Mark Pierson and Cathy Kirkpatrick.

Less rigidly organised, congregationally structured churches like Baptists were sometimes more able to make changes. They could experiment in worship and church organisation more quickly. They also, however, had more conservatives in their number who disapproved of new ventures.

The Presbyterian church in New Zealand tried its Theological Hall's Principal for heresy in 1969, so intellectual questioning had been overt for a while before the 1990s. I thought about that moment, which I'd watched from afar as a teenager. I could now see it was an intellectual doctrinal battle between conservatives and liberals. They were scrapping over modernist interpretations of Christianity's core propositions. Unfortunately, it seemed to also have stiffened conservatives' resolve to not let theological 'standards' slip, a resolve not much abated in the early 21st century.

These debates were a 20th century version of 19th century heresy trials in Scotland. I remembered reading of one Presbyterian academic, William Robertson Smith, being questioned in 1881. He'd stated Moses didn't write the first five books of the First Testament. This showed how biblical criticism threatened traditional views. These traditional views were held in the church, but not always in the academy.

Smith's own teachers and his current Principal defended him on the grounds that discussion of broader ideas should be allowed without personal penalty. He was later deposed as a teacher in the church, though not as a minister.

I remembered the case well. Robertson Smith was writing articles for the first edition of the *Encyclopaedia Britannica*. It tickled my sense of humour that he seemed to be committing heresy by alphabet. He wrote articles on 'Angels', then 'Bible,' then 'Moses.' No sooner was one trial completed, than another article was published. It must have been a tense time for the church as well as for Smith. The trials were followed in detail in New Zealand. Reporting of them in New Zealand Presbyterian church periodicals happened surprisingly quickly after the events in Scotland.

We experienced contemporary 'post-' movements in the late 20th and early 21st centuries. These were responses to the crumbling of the modern project. Its 'onward and upward,' 'making-progress-all-the-time' approach encouraged a triumphalist Christianity which many now reject. Postmodern critique distrusts meta-narratives and assumptions of steady progress towards perfection.

Hindsight shows that the entire modern perspective in the Christian project was a false enthusiasm. It was bolstered by fear that Christendom was in its final throes. It had overtones rather like the panic induced by the fall of the Roman Empire centuries before.

Yet Christian perspectives remain in our general, though secular, society. In New Zealand I've observed many people in politics, not-for-profits and writers of different genres whose roots are in organised Christianity. Many later broke free of its narrower frameworks.

However, values learned in Sunday schools and church schools were imbued in them. These refugees from organised Christianity are significant contributors to a compassionate civility in parts of New Zealand society. For example, the third woman prime minister of the country, Jacinda Ardern, has a Mormon background. This may well have contributed to her urging the country to 'be kind' during the Covid 19 pandemic.

New Zealand, in 2021, still needs to grapple with prevalent racism, sexism, and grinding poverty for many. Conversations about these issues are now being held in the public space more overtly than before. The pandemic is showing up inconsistencies which had been hidden earlier. New alliances between formerly separate groupings of people are beginning to get traction on difficult issues.

In this postmodern setting I've been watching so-called 'liberal' and 'progressive' Christians. I am increasingly saddened by the way they discard Christian traditions, which seem to embarrass them as they become more liberally minded. I wonder if they are still influenced by the confident dominance of modernist thinking in science and religion, which arose just as their cohort became religious and societal leaders. They haven't noticed that since then, postmodern questioning has led to a variety of positions being acceptable. Attitudes are now more fluid and flexible than during the mid-20th-century's hard-line science vs religion wars.

In my view, progressives and liberals seem to frequently replace seeking spirituality with an activist stance in social justice. Several secular causes have benefitted from this infusion of energy, but I feel these individuals are missing out on numinous power. They do not seem to comprehend the underlying flow of the spirit I imagine in the metaphor of the aquifers. It is for me, a compulsive call which I still feel strongly.

12 — Can psychology or philosophy help with the journey?

It was the following Friday when Hope and I met again over flat whites in the coffee-infused atmosphere of *The Cup*. I shared some of the historical reminiscing her email had started for me. She asked what writers were important to my journey now.

"I'm incredibly grateful for insights I've gained through a Jungian slant," I replied. "Jung's significance is particularly well described by David Tacey. His work on Australian spirituality and especially university students' spirituality was a first foundation.[55] His latest book is *Beyond Literal Belief: The Bible as Metaphor*."[56]

"My copy of that arrived the other day," said Hope. "I'm really enjoying his explanations of myth."

"He's good on that. I also find his analysis in another book of his, *Darkening Spirit*[57] very astute, though a little frightening. He sees a darkening spirit spreading globally. He names it a reaction of the shadow side of individuals and societies. He reckons they have more licence now that religion and religious symbols have lost power. It's a global theological version of 'while the cat's away the mice will play' I suppose!"

"Well, think of that riot at the US Capitol prior to President Biden's inauguration in 2021. It was a shocking display of weird behaviour. Is that the kind of thing he means?" asked Hope.

"I think so. That was a tangible expression of such confusion and darkness. It crystallised many people's unease with the lies endemic in the outgoing presidency. It starkly illustrates how things can go horribly wrong. Especially when individual's egos become overinflated as their response to the collapse of Christendom," I said.

"You mean like in that Edinger 'tepee' diagram?" asked Hope.

"You have been paying attention! Yes indeed," I teased.

Hope's face was serious. "There've been shocking happenings in the American political scene during Trump's four years. The worst is collusion between right-wing evangelicals and President Trump's 'alternative facts.'"

"Unfortunately, that's a perfect illustration of what can go wrong. It's caused by spirit being buried beneath other organisational and power-brokering concerns. I found it symbolically significant that incoming President Joe Biden cited Abraham Lincoln. It was a piece about bringing his whole soul to the role. This is what I found in an online article about it. I tapped on my tablet and turned the screen to Hope.

> "My whole soul is in it," the new president quoted from Lincoln's 1863 Emancipation Proclamation. Biden continued, "Today, on this January day, my whole soul is in this – bringing America together, uniting our people, uniting our nation. And I ask every American to join me in this cause."[58]

"'Soul' is exactly what has become buried and missing in the religion I was taught. It is also buried in a secular society," I said.

"Do you mean the soul which goes to heaven?" asked Hope with a puzzled frown.

"No, not an eternal soul, good only for admission to heaven. I mean the soul which is that part of us deeper than mind and emotions. Depth psychology á la Jung is key for me. His work exposes the insidious way ego can twist even an honourable framework, (like the Christian Church), causing people in it to be dominating and controlling."

"Ego-driven lives can turn even the best frameworks into the opposite of the truth, honour and integrity they were designed to protect. All the ego wants is to please and be approved. We human beings rate acceptance in the group as all important. In that way, ego-driven lives cause inauthentic behaviour," I said.

Hope nodded. "I've seen that happening," she murmured.

"From Jungian thought, I'm learning that when the Self, (capital S), is allowed to emerge and speak, be listened to and be heeded, it leads us on a different route. The Self is a guide to the journey we've been discussing. You could say that the questioning described in Stage four is the Self beginning to be heard."

"How does that work out in practice?" asked Hope.

"I'm still struggling with that. I've been asking myself whether there's one Great Myth we must follow," I said.

"That doesn't sound any different from what you've been questioning. It sounds like that modern meta-narrative stuff which you've been saying we should move on from," commented Hope. This young woman was sharp.

"I think you're right. That's the conclusion I think I'm coming to as well. I've decided we need to simply encounter the reality of life as it is. I think though, that our encounters with life need to change in character. I know I need to interact with life differently from before. I need to do it in a more mythical and mystical way," I said.

"It's something like looking inside each life event, even each day, for its gift, for the numinosity within it. That way we will find the God-within-life and the God-within-our-Self. I'm wondering if the mythical journey is more like a verb than a noun. We're not so much following The Myth but making the myth as we go along. It's a little like Sam and Frodo made the story of carrying the Ring."

"Each circumstance we encounter can be thought of as a loom. On it and in it we can weave a whole new tapestry. The result is a tapestry which is a symbolic, mythical, and mystical way of seeing the world, ourselves and our fellow human beings," I said.

"That sounds complicated, but good too," said Hope. "I think when you actually are weaving it all together, it might be simpler than talking about it."

"Yes, I should remember my own warning to you that this is not easy to explain!" I said.

"It's like we're invited to enter a new space. Kind of the hero's journey. *The Carpenter and the Unbuilder* suggests it is challenging because of the vulnerability it asks of us. Still, it's a gentle, quiet way. More about compassion than compression, more about receiving as well as giving. It's about strength within, rather than power over," I said.

"Yes!" exclaimed Hope. "Yes!" her eyes sparkled with the delight of discovery.

"When I was looking up some Jungian concepts the other day, I found David Tacey, who said Jung called religion 'anything that provides escape from egocentricity, relief from the mundane.'"[59]

"Anything that provides escape from egocentricity, relief from the mundane," Hope repeated, scribbling a note on her napkin. "That's good."

"Tacey says, 'Our world's not only ego-centric but also terribly, terribly concrete and functional. We're obsessed with the material and the mundane. We're focused on earthbound popularity and power.' I've got the article on my phone, let me read this bit to you," I said.

> The ego is a prison, caught in time, space and rationality. We need to leave this mental prison behind from time to time, and on a regular basis. What can get us out? Poetry, love, sex, therapy, passion, nature, ritual, ceremony, music, empathy, compassion, and 'feeling with' the world.[60]

Hope read the words over to herself, her lips moving silently.

"So the 'journey' we've been talking about may be more about finding a 'parallel universe.' A kind of different universe where we still inhabit the world, yet our mind, heart, and soul look at it from a radically different perspective?" she asked.

"That's right. The trust which the Carpenter couldn't develop at first, but later did, is a trust that whatever turns up, we can live it in a mythically knowledgeable way. If we take the first step, the journey will come to us. The whole approach needs a flexibility which older Christian creeds and doctrinal frameworks don't allow for," I replied.

"I haven't heard a lot about Jung, nor much at all about depth psychology. When did it get started and why?" asked Hope.

"Depth Psychology got going during, and probably because of, World Wars I and II. It was developing as the modern Christian project was on the wane in the western world. I don't think that was a coincidence, but rather, one of those fascinating synchronistic juxtapositions of events. This article gives some background which you might find useful. I'll get us more coffee while you read it."

"OK. Another flat white for me please." Hope bent over my phone.

> There is an emptiness in our culture that all of the social and economic security in the world could not cure. To Jung, it was the religious impulse – inherent in the sacred nature of the psyche (soul) – that has the potential to heal the restlessness and material craving so prevalent in our time, and provide us with living symbols, rituals, and rites of passage to meaning-make life's transitions and encounter a world *ensouled*.[61]

When I returned, Hope looked up. "I love that bit at the end," she said, "where Jung talks about the religious impulse."

"It's a good summary. I've been thinking for some time that depth psychology provides a useful language. It's intelligible to post-Enlightenment thinkers. It's a discipline intellectually respectable enough to capture their attention. I'm getting more and more convinced depth psychology could be a new 'language' for 21st century seekers to talk about the sacred and the religious. It includes symbols and metaphors as part of its vocabulary. It takes seriously how important these are to our psyche (soul)," I said.

Hope looked interested. "Tell me more," she said.

"I came across the story of Paul Tillich when I was teaching a theologians paper for ordinands last year. He produced an important piece of theological interpretation during and after World War II," I began.

"I've heard that name before. Dad quoted Tillich quite a lot," said Hope.

"He would. Your Dad would be part of the generation of ministers influenced quite heavily by Tillich's work. Paul Tillich was sacked from his academic post in 1933 by the Third Reich. He was encouraged by friends to move to America. In his systematic theology, he used the still relatively new idea of existential philosophy to explain theology. He correlated Christian insights with existential thought. He not only appealed to academia, but his radio talks were also extremely popular throughout America. Like depth psychology, the rise of existential philosophy was a product of the times. It suited a period when religious dogma was being increasingly challenged."

"What exactly is existential philosophy?" asked Hope. "It was brought up in one of my theology papers, but I never quite grasped what it was about."

I take a breath. "Let's see if I can sum up Existentialism in a few sentences! The key to Existentialism is that it focuses on a person's actual thoughts, feelings, and actions. It is concerned with meaning and existence, who we are and how to 'be' in this world. 'Existential angst' is the anxiety we feel when life seems meaningless. The first existential philosophers lived at the end of the 19th and into the 20th century. Compared with other philosophers, they emphasised actual human experience, not abstractions."

"Who were they?" asked Hope.

"Let me see…," I said.

"Have you heard of Soren Kierkegaard? He could be thought of as founding existentialism. He emphasised it was individuals themselves who gave meaning to their lives. He believed we were the ones responsible for living our lives authentically."

"Jean Paul Sartre, heard of him?" I asked. Hope nodded.

"Sartre was perhaps the key existentialist philosopher. He was influenced by what he read while in a POW camp during World War II," I said.

"Any women in the group?" asked Hope.

"Simone de Beauvoir was one woman associated with the French existentialists," I replied.

"So existentialism and depth psychology started around the same time, give or take a decade or two?" asked Hope.

"Yes. Jung works within psychology rather than philosophy, but the Jungian emphasis on inner development aligns with key existentialist themes. They are both about bringing meaning to life by developing your inner life. They are about exercising freedom. They encourage us to work on all the ways we naturally deceive ourselves, so we can gain clarity," I said.

"That makes me think of Jesus, in a way," said Hope thoughtfully. "He encouraged developing our inner life through story and metaphor. Remember his reply to the Pharisees about taxes? He gave Jews, whose land was occupied by Romans, permission to exercise creative freedom. He certainly challenged self-deception when he told only those without sin to cast the first stone. You know, in that case of adultery he was presented with," she said.

"You're right. The positive impact of Jesus on the world was in large part because of the authenticity he showed in such moments. Inauthentic people do not make a lasting impact, except as objects of infamy," I added.

"You know, I've been thinking," said Hope as she began to pack up her things. "This suggests that a mythical approach is more effective over time than a doctrinal one. Doctrines are written down and set in concrete, as it were. They're less able to flex and morph as our lives change."

"That's true. If we meet life events just as they are, and apply a mythical perspective to them, we automatically have flexible ways to live in an increasingly flexible world," I replied.

"Bend it like Beckham!" said Hope, as she hoisted her bag on her shoulder and laughed her way out the door.

13 — Who are the priests and prophets of the journey?

Hope was in a pensive mood when we next met. We got our coffees and made our way to a spot in the corner of the outdoor courtyard. It was a beautiful early autumn day. Sitting in the fresh air was a bonus in the middle of a busy week.

"What's up, Hope. You seem quiet today," I prompted.

"I liked our session last week. I'm going to look at existentialism and depth psychology more. But, it seems so complicated. How could I explain all that to others who want to know what I'm getting into? Charlie said yesterday that it seemed more complicated than regular church. He asked why do I feel I have to get into all this stuff?" said Hope.

"And it matters what Charlie thinks?" I asked.

Hope blushed. "Yes … well… it just does," she finished in a rush. "But it's not just Charlie. Sometimes it seems to be so enormous and yet all so inexplicable. I don't know how to describe it."

"What does Charlie do?" I asked, an idea forming in my head.

"He's doing a really interesting double major, a B.A. / LLB. Music and Law," answered Hope.

"Do you think it's the rational, lawyer part of him that's finding it difficult? What about his more lyrical musical side? You see, the leaders in this new journey are not theologians or dogmatic," I said.

"The new leaders and prophets are poets, with their intuition and creativity and metaphors. It's no accident that depth psychology and existential philosophy are the two branches of those disciplines which are the most helpful. They are both also the most open to emotion and human experience," I said.

"You mean this journey is more about intuition than intellect?" asked Hope.

"Something like that. Though our intellect is really helpful for us to discern what is spiritual and what is simply wacky!" I replied.

"I love poetry. I feel really grounded when I read it. It calms me down, takes me deep inside somehow. Charlie likes poetry too. He's doing the rock music option in the Music Department. The lyrics are really important to him as well as the music," said Hope.

"Rock music lyrics often have great psychological and existential meaning. You might find Charlie relates intuitively to what depth psychology and existentialism offers, while finding the explanations not interesting at all."

"He might understand more of what you're discovering by reading poetry which expresses the essence of the journey. You could try him on *The Carpenter and the Unbuilder* too if you haven't already. It's prose, but it's very mythological, poetical prose," I said.

"Which poets have you found helpful? Which ones show us the spiritual way?" asked Hope.

"Mary Oliver is a Canadian poet who involves nature a lot in her work. She catches something of the importance of an individual reaction to life events in her famous poem *Wild Geese*. The poem always soothes me with its advice that I do not have to follow the rules all the time, but can relax into my human self, especially my body. At the end of the poem, she uses the image of wild geese flying their v-shaped formation to suggest that the universe is naming our role in the world as key members of the human (and creaturely) community."[62]

"Oh, I must get a copy of that." Hope grabs her own napkin and starts scribbling Mary's name and the poem title. "What other poems of hers should I try?"

"There's *Summer Day* and *I Worried*. They might be a good start,"[63] I said.

"Any others?" asked Hope.

"Our own New Zealand writer Joy Cowley has some lovely reflective stuff. Her spiritual language is quite conventional, but her ideas are not. She's got several books… let me see… *Aotearoa Psalms, Psalms for the Road, Psalms Down-Under* and *Come and See*. Most of them are published by Catholic Book Supplies or Pleroma. One phrase of hers which I love is in a Nativity poem she writes about Christ being born 'in the rough stable of our lives.'"

"I've seen her stuff used in church. She does have some great Advent and Christmas poems, doesn't she?" said Hope.

"Carol Ann Duffy is the poet laureate in Britain," I said. "She names fleeting moments of life which for her are prayers of different length and intensity. In one poem, she even includes the sound of someone playing piano scales and names of coastal locations which toll each night in the weather forecast for the UK shipping channels."[64]

"I found out about that poem from Dave Tomlinson. Charlie might like Dave Tomlinson's writing. He talks about music written in so-called secular musical circles which speaks to him of whatever God is, in his latest book, *'Black Sheep and Prodigals.'* He likes the music and lyrics of Nick Cave. Charlie might relate to him. I've got *Black Sheep* in my bag. You can borrow it if you like. This is the bit I mean," I said.

I turned to the page and read:

> Has God written any good tunes lately? Yes of course. But you won't necessarily hear them in church (though you might). Wherever I look in the world I discover divine revelation – at a music gig or on iTunes, in a poetry book or an art gallery, on TV or at the theatre, in the playfulness of a child or the liberated imagination of a grown-up. It enriches my life, and sometimes calls me to a different life.[65]

"We need to live life by applying our intuition. We grow by using our imagination. We learn by welcoming mystery. Seeking mythological themes threading their way through our lives is the way to feed our soul or psyche. When we do, we nourish the inner self, so it grows stronger. It's then more able to accompany us each day in a way we can hear and feel, sometimes see and touch," I said.

Hope looked thoughtful.

"Penny for your thoughts?" I asked.

"I suppose the journey is more mythological than dogmatic," replied Hope. "That means we won't be able to nail it all down into one of those huge confessional things we've talked about. I can't give Charlie that kind of evidence or description. We can only ever reflect and muse and wonder and sketch the outline of what's happening."

"The word for what happens on the journey is that lovely old word 'ineffable' – unable to be worded. The dictionary translates it as 'too great or extreme to be expressed or described in words.' Sounds a lot like rock music lyrics to me!" I exclaimed.

"I like that… ineffable…," mused Hope.

We sat in silence for a few moments. It made me think of the Carpenter and the Unbuilder sitting in the carpenter's front yard, letting the mystery of the path wrap itself around even their waiting. Had I been an adequate Unbuilder for Hope? It seemed to me she was braver than the carpenter and had been walking the journey with courage and grace.

More slowly than usual, Hope gathered her gear and rose to go.

"Thanks so much," she said. "See you!"

"See you," I echoed. "Go well."

There was more I could have said, but Hope seemed to have an instinct about how much she could absorb at any one time. I pondered what had been coming to mind as we talked.

Since my eyes have opened more, I now see that mythological themes recur all the time. Steeped in bible stories from my youth, I can sometimes recognise them from echoes of those old bible stories and characters. It's no accident that biblical phrases and allusions have entered the general western English vocabulary; 'Doubting Thomas,' 'cast the first stone,' 'Judas,' 'Promised Land,' 'lion's den,' 'prodigal,' 'lost sheep,' 'Greater love has no one than this, than to lay down one's life for their friends.' These words and phrases stick with us, and enter our vocabulary because there are Big Ideas or the Big Story behind them.

Many biblical stories ring true for people who are not church goers because they are about authentic human experience. Because of that, we recognise within our own depths emotions and fears, other people's experiences at pivotal moments.

Taking a symbolic approach to the spiritual journey helps. As a traveller I often see moments in which awe, gratitude and deep pleasure are appropriate. When I'm intentional about my travelling, I notice more. The more attention I pay, the more I am mindful in the present moment.

When I am an intentional traveller, I'm prepared to take time to dwell. I reflect and meditate before moving on in the ever-flowing stream of life. We've had various lockdowns and restrictions on our movements during the global pandemic. They've given rise to many moments in which we've all noticed more about our world and those with whom we live.

For some people, there has been more time to watch seasons change. Others appreciate more when snowdrops push through still cold earth. It has been easier to notice the small bird inhabiting the garden or to really see a sunset.

Writers and poets note that these apparently mundane moments have the aura of 'God' in them. This understanding sees 'God' as spirit, energy, or life force. In this understanding, we intuit 'God' as a numinosity, as the holy one, the creative force that flows through us all.

Elizabeth Barrett Browning expressed this. She lived years before we started this contemporary rediscovering of the ubiquity of the presence of the sacred. I have long loved four of her lines from a larger poem.

> "Earth's crammed with heaven,
> And every common bush afire with God,
> But only he who sees takes off his shoes;
> The rest sit round and pluck blackberries."

When I investigated the origin of this short quote, I found that the longer poem, *Aurora Leigh,* from which these lines come, argues that there is an indivisible tie between the spiritual and the material. If this tie is broken, the poem argues, it makes the material 'impossible.' It also means the spiritual is unable to be appreciated.

> …Natural things
> And spiritual,—who separates those two
> In art, in morals, or the social drift
> Tears up the bond of nature and brings death,
> Paints futile pictures, writes unreal verse,
> Leads vulgar days, deals ignorantly with men,
> Is wrong, in short, at all points. We divide
> This apple of life, and cut it through the pips,—
> The perfect round which fitted Venus' hand
> Has perished as utterly as if we ate
> Both halves. Without the spiritual, observe,
> The natural's impossible,—no form,
> No motion: without sensuous, spiritual
> Is inappreciable,—no beauty or power:

I was trying to do what I had told Hope was impossible. I was attempting to describe to myself what is going on here. It seems to me it is something about a constant flow of energy.

One energy stream is from ancient mythological stories, in books such as the Bible, towards the actual events of our own lives now. The numinosity of the symbolism of these stories, which appears silly to rational students of history, can spark within us imaginative and creative ways to live in the world.

The other flow of energy, as Elizabeth Barrett Browning suggested, is from our actual material world. It is about the world's forms and shapes, colours and hues, the life within in them, plant, animal, and human with all their variety and changing developments. From a leaf floating on a lake, to a solar system in the night sky, we can reflect on these images and feelings. That leads to our developing metaphors which nourish soul. If we pay attention, it becomes a constant flow to and from, from and to. The spirit in perpetual motion connects us, accepts us and guides our way.

I lingered, coffee cooling in my cup. I was oblivious to the hiss of the espresso machine from the coffee shop coming through the open window. I could no longer hear the chatter around me. I allowed myself to enter that parallel myth-making universe. Things shifted and became clear. I enjoyed a rare moment of epiphanous peace.

14 — Leading the way to re-enchantment

It was a few months before Hope and I met face-to-face again. We'd been keeping in touch through email. I knew she'd found a spiritual director who understood her uncommon spiritual journey with this 'new' emphasis. I heard from time to time of discoveries she was making. I had a rough idea of books she'd been reading. She seemed happy in her own skin.

Hope still attended church, but I knew she'd been following online resources too. Both her generation, and older 'travellers' find the internet a good way to connect with like-minded seekers.

One Zoom meeting, a single Facebook post or a YouTube video could draw people from around the world. A small garden shed in Somerset could 'hold' over 100 participants.[66] One person from their home office desk can curate and send out challenging poetry, art and music, along with wise words. These offerings can nourish souls who can't find a local church nearby where they can experience authentic connection. A northern hemisphere Zoom meeting at lunchtime can host antipodeans joining the meeting in the dark of a southern night.[67] Moments of beauty can be recorded and replayed again and again.

I'm intrigued by a group of people who met first in London seeking a replacement for church. Calling themselves Sunday Assembly, the gatherings were started in 2013 by two stand-up comedians. They wanted to create a gathering which did not include God but was still like church. First, they met in a deconsecrated church, then in a public hall. During the pandemic they met online. Attendances range from 100 to 600.

Such 'pop-up' ventures organise and finance themselves with merchandising and online donations. Their oversight board states this on their website:

> We are Sunday Assembly's Board of Trustees and responsible
> for running the charity. In addition to making sure we comply
> with laws and look after everyone, with the help and support
> of our community we also steer the strategic direction of
> the charity. We put the structures in place to make sure that

everything Sunday Assembly does is done in a safe, ethical and legal way.[68]

Other Sunday Assemblies have sprung up. There are 40 throughout the world, including in the UK, Australia, Germany, Ireland, Netherlands, New Zealand and the United States. I wonder what will happen if the groups become more numerous. Will a central control ever be part of their ethos? No doubt a new generation will do things differently.

Wikipedia describes the gatherings as "mostly for non-religious people who want a similar communal experience to a religious church." Volunteers organise gatherings. Researchers have studied this grouping looking at how millennials achieve community. Since its beginning, community values had been named: "Live Better, Help Often and Wonder More." These have been expanded in what you could call a simple creed.

- Live Better: We aim to provide inspiring, thought-provoking, and practical ideas that help people to live the lives they want to lead and be the people they want to be.

- Help Often: Assemblies are communities of action building lives of purpose, encouraging us all to help anyone who needs it to support each other.

- Wonder More: Hearing talks, singing as one, listening to readings and even playing games helps us to connect with each other and the awesome world we live in.

And they enthusiastically add:

Sunday Assembly so much more than just a wonderful event twice a month. It's about each and every person who is part of the community and us all living our lives to the fullest.[69]

This kind of group is more organised and structured than a lone video-blogger in a shed at the bottom of their garden. The blogger asks for donations in a laid-back way. The Sunday Assembly community have skills or have purchased skills in website creation, merchandise production, retailing, and event organisation.

The website of the spin-off New Zealand Sunday Assembly based in Christchurch has a clear motto, mission and vision expressed with confidence.

The Sunday Assembly is a godless congregation that celebrates life.

- Our motto: live better, help often, wonder more.
- Our mission: to help everyone find and fulfil their full potential.
- Our vision: a godless congregation in every town, city and village that wants one.

The Christchurch website makes 10 statements which clarify their existence and ethos. The tone is more definite than the original London Assembly's wordage. I wonder if the New Zealand Sunday Assembly faced opposition which made this explicit definition necessary. I also wonder whether convinced atheists are keen that the Assembly does not slip into a quasi-religious style.

The Sunday Assembly

- Is 100% celebration of life. We are born from nothing and go to nothing. Let's enjoy it together.
- Has no doctrine. We have no set texts so we can make use of wisdom from all sources.
- Has no deity. We don't do supernatural, but we also won't tell you you're wrong if you do.
- Is radically inclusive. Everyone is welcome, regardless of their beliefs – this is a place of love that is open and accepting.
- Is free to attend, not-for-profit and volunteer run. We ask for donations to cover our costs and support our community work.
- Has a community mission. Through our Action Heroes (you!), we will be a force for good.
- Is independent. We do not accept sponsorship or promote outside businesses, organisations or services
- Is here to stay. With your involvement, The Sunday Assembly will make the world a better place
- We won't won't [sic] tell you how to live, but will try to help you do it as well as you can
- And remember point 1… The Sunday Assembly is a celebration of the one life we know we have.[70]

This eclectic mix of statements distances the group from organised religion. It is like, I mused with a wry smile, Protestant confessions of faith creating distinctions between themselves and continuing catholic faith in the 16th century.

I noted their lofty goals and confidence that Sunday Assembly will make the world a better place and its determination to do good through community mission. There's a certainty expressed on their website that attending the Sunday Assembly will be an energising experience, even a 'touch' of the transcendent is on offer.

> What should you expect from a Sunday Assembly event?

> Just by being with us you should be energised, vitalised, restored, repaired, refreshed, and recharged. No matter what the subject of the Assembly, it will solace worries, provoke kindness and inject a touch of transcendence into the everyday.

> But life can be tough… It is. Sometimes bad things happen to good people, we have moments of weakness or life just isn't fair. We want The Sunday Assembly to be a house of love and compassion, where, no matter what your situation, you are welcomed, accepted and loved.

> Most of all, have fun, be nice and join in.[71]

I can't find evidence on their website or Facebook page of the community mission of 'action heroes.' Perhaps they are more of a concept than an organised thing.

Globally, the Sunday Assembly movement celebrated its eighth anniversary in January 2021; the anniversary of the first OG (original gathering) in the UK. They enjoyed a "Yule lockdown rockdown" at the end of 2020 at the winter solstice in a Zoom gathering, with contributions from ten Sunday Assembly chapters worldwide.

Is this the 'church' of the future, overtly rejecting the supernatural? In their own words they were: "… all the best bits of church, but with no religion, and awesome songs!"

Is this still a spiritual journey, or determinedly something different? One thing I've learned on my own journey is that you don't need to go to church to be moral or ethical. The church does not have a monopoly on morality.

These communities, on their websites anyway, convey the importance they place on being compassionate and conscious of the world around them. On their websites they don't seem to have any accompanying judgmental attitudes or narrow fundamentalism.

The 2021 new year newsletter from the Board to the London-based original Sunday Assembly reflects the life of the community during 2020. They are excited that two fundraising campaigns in 2020 raised just over £20,000. Securing grants was also important.

Interestingly, they believe work is needed on 'accessibility, diversity and inclusion' within the Sunday Assembly community.

> During our annual picnic season in August, when we could actually meet in parks again, so many people volunteered their time and energy to make our in-person gatherings possible! Many went above and beyond to ensure others weren't alone during this difficult time by hosting online meetups, social activities, Live Better groups, and even online gatherings on Christmas Day and Boxing Day… In moving our assemblies online, we also realised that we could and should make this part of Sunday Assembly London's usual activities when we return to the post-pandemic world. And we are excited to tell you that towards the end of 2020, we successfully secured £7,000 in funding from the National Lottery Community Fund to make this happen!

> This grant means that in addition to live streaming our events when we return to Conway Hall, the funding will also help us improve the way we operate. In 2021, we'll start making strides toward strengthening our infrastructure, with particular emphasis on our volunteers and governance. We are also going to kickstart some much-needed work on accessibility, diversity, and inclusion in our community by hosting workshops, requesting your involvement, and asking for your feedback.[72]

Realities of time and space, funding and practising inclusivity, which the church also struggles with, are still realities, no matter how loosely and collaboratively any new venture is organised. I reflect wryly about all the nasty cracks the church suffers because it asks its members to give money to the cause. These new ventures just ask for money online. The bad press the church gets for its exclusivity at times also comes to mind. Sunday Assemblies are facing the same problems.

Within the period which Phyllis Tickle described as the Great Emergence, a variety of options have emerged, approximately 500 years after the Reformation. Greater use of the internet to connect people during the coronavirus pandemic has allowed these groups to become more visible internationally.

I wondered what choices Hope would make in the end about her own journey and her vocation. I found it interesting that her original questions about training for the ministry of the church had not been re-asked after our discussion had come to a natural end. I didn't think assisting in the antiquarian bookshop would keep her satisfied for long, however. She had a questing mind and would want to embrace a career that kept her thinking at the edges of a lot of different areas.

I saw through our emails that Hope and Charlie were becoming more of an item in recent months. A relationship always influences a person's life choices regarding vocation. I was keen that Hope would find her true metier before she committed to a long-term relationship with Charlie, and make sure she had a good sense of herself going in.

Charlie too, I knew, had his questions. He'd been brought up in a liberal Christian household. He approached spirituality from a different angle. I knew he and Hope had long discussions. Together, I was sure they would continue to search and seek. I thought they had the potential to become a remarkably interesting couple from whom others would learn much.

The door opened and Hope came in on a gust of wind and autumn leaves. The year had morphed into autumn without my really noticing. Her cheeks were flushed with the cold air. I held up my cup and she waved and joined the queue at the counter.

"Sorry to be late, but I've just come from an interview," she said as soon as she reached our table. "It's a not-for-profit which is working on a co-housing project a couple of blocks away."

"That sounds interesting," I said, pleased I had been right about the bookshop not holding her for long. "Do you mean SHALOM, that new development on the corner of Moore and Devon Street?"

"That's the one. Charlie and I joined the planning group a few months ago. They need a paid coordinator to keep volunteers connected and communicating well. This particular co-housing project is part of a bigger scheme they run. The whole thing includes foodbanks, community gardens, advocacy, town planning activism and well-health initiatives like mental health work." She mentioned the name of an international not-for-profit known for its humanitarian work with a spiritual ethos.

She blushed as she continued, "Charlie and I have applied for one of the houses in the co-housing unit. It should be ready this coming spring."

I was fascinated by this turn of events. "So, Charlie and you are going to live together?"

"Yes." Were her eyes a little starry? "He's graduating next month. He's just been appointed to a position in a law firm which does a lot of advocacy work, some of it pro bono. It all fits together, really. Guess what? We hope we might be able to run a spirituality group in the communal meeting room, or somewhere nearby."

"A spirituality group. Sounds great! Any ideas yet on the format?" I asked.

"We're not sure. Definitely a gathering with high levels of respect and trust. Fairly informal. Input each time followed by Q & A or discussion. We also want to experiment. We'll try contemporary liturgy which avoids old clichés. We tried something out last week with just a few friends. I'll email it to you. (See Appendix 4) We'll get back in touch when we're properly set up. You'd be a great speaker on the days we get someone in from outside, if you have the time."

I watched Hope's animated face as she talked about her plans and dreams. She had found her stride. She knew how to seek and search for herself. Already she was thinking of helping others to find the way too.

I thought again of the Carpenter and the Unbuilder waiting in the yard of the Carpenter's latest refuge from the journey:

> Slowly it began to seem as though they were already on the journey. As that feeling grew and grew, it suddenly didn't seem like any decision needed to be made; it just happened. With a deep sense of freedom, they were off.[73]

This is the end of Hope's beginning

Appendix — 1 Creeds

Creed for an Easter People

Death does not put a full stop on our experience
We live on in memory, through DNA,
in artefacts we leave behind.
We live on through the influence we have had on others
– for good or ill.

Jesus lives on in us through
the influence of his teaching, wise and thoughtful
the caring behind his compassion, shown to many
the view he held of justice as the right of all.

We rejoice that new life continually springs forth
phoenix-like from the ashes of life,
as seedlings flourish in the humus of the earth,
the old transformed within the grave of the chrysalis
into new forms previously unknown
which fill the world with beauty and delight.

Creed About Love

We believe all creation is good;
that in each of us
is the divine spark of Love
and within us all are
a thousand possibilities and potentialities
for both good and evil.

We believe we are invited
to enter the ongoing struggle
of bringing to birth Love in our world
in more places and within more people;
of facilitating and celebrating
the deep union of sacred and secular.

We value Jesus who gives hope to ordinary people;
turning the regular into the special
showing the way of transformation
crashing through any boundaries
which separate us from Life.

We welcome the Spirit
who can never be confined,
but appears in the most unexpected of places
always leading humankind
in the dance of life wherever it may lead.

A South Canterbury Creed

We believe in God, known to us in many ways;
by braided rivers threading through the rolling downs
in sunlit tussock on snow etched hills,
in small waves washing on the sweeping Bay.

We believe in Jesus known to us in many ways;
through a life showing his love for all,
in parables that puzzle and challenge us,
in actions which make us gasp in pain and wonder.

We believe in the Spirit known to us in mystery;
As daunting as the nor-west wind,
yet gentle as a candle flame,
breaking us open with warmth and energy.

We believe in the Church,
this small vessel of fragile clay into which God entrusts
the many truths describing the divine
and prodigally splashes love which does not end,
where we are baptised in trust and faith.

We believe that our belief is only true
when seen in action;
calming anxious minds
feeding fractured families
bringing faith in darkness;
Actions for which we depend upon the grace of God
to call us, to empower and to guide.

Timaru, New Zealand

Appendix — 2 Affirmations

Affirmation of Faith

Events often have ineffable quality
impossible to capture in words
Ancient women and men experienced more
than words on scroll or page ever detail;
So we know scripture comes to us
filtered through minds and hearts,
contexts and circumstances.

In the events of our own lives
we can be moved by feather-light touches of grace
or tossed about in a maelstrom of meaning
or pain twists our gut in rictus agony;
So we know divine words form in us
without sound or vocabulary,
shaped by who we are now.

Spoken or unspoken, the Word forms in us now
as it formed long ago in people like us, yet not like us.
We sense its truth in feelings too deep for words
or thoughts too complicated for grammar;
So we know the Word is all around us and within
In this, in all of us, is the Word.
Thanks be given.

Affirmation of Wilderness

We affirm there is a journey to be followed
through the mazes of our lives;
a journey which can wind through wilderness
that lonely, awe-inspiring space
carved in solitude,
formed by silence.

We take heart that in wilderness
we inhabit a place Jesus walked before us;
that both wilderness and marketplace
are one in him,
and can be brought together in one unity
within us too, at the very deepest level.

We affirm that wilderness is
an integral part of a loving Creation,
that on desert paths we are accompanied by Christ
and that the Spirit's impetus
invites us to transformation within

Lent 1

Affirming the Waste of Perfume

Like drops of perfume, our acts can be small
yet like its fragrance, fill the space around us.
We know even a small act different from expected practice
can expose us to ridicule and shame.

Yet, the fragrance of that offering can also linger
not only for that one night, but through centuries,
sweetening difficult, dark moments for others,
far removed in time and space but not in circumstance,
the congruence of the moment creating a bond
with those who also wish to give what seems so little
and yet means so much.

We affirm small offerings

We affirm brave movements made by frightened people
out of overpowering love.

We affirm courage in all its forms
and gratefully breathe in the fragrance of Love.

Lent 5

Appendix — 3 Great Prayer of Thanksgiving

Great Prayer of Thanksgiving

The Spirit be with you
And also with you
Lift up your hearts.
We lift them up
Let us give thanks
It is right to offer thanks and praise
It is indeed right to give thanks,
With the whole created universe
We praise the unfailing gift of life,
We give thanks that we have been made human.

Love came among us in Jesus Christ,
Who makes all things new, not only renewing us,
but bringing the promise of a renewed creation,
a new heaven and a new earth,
with reconciliation of all peoples.

Therefore, with those who have walked this earth before us
Whether by belief or by other paths,
with all those who share this planet with us now
its vast oceans and tall mountains,
its serene lakes and flowing rivers,
stormy moments and myriad creatures, joyfully we say:

Holy, holy, holy, Love, Life, and Energy
Earth and sea and sky and all that lives
declare your presence and your glory.

Jesus, our brother,
made known to us afresh each time in the breaking of bread;
who, on the night he was handed over to be killed,
when he was with his friends, much like us,
took bread, gave thanks, broke it and said:
'This is my body which is for you;
do this to remember me"
In the same way also the cup after supper saying
'This cup represents the new covenant;
do this whenever you drink it, to remember me.'

Appendix — 4
Hope and Charlie's Experimental Liturgy

Hi f & m,

This was our first go at creating a gathering format. We're not sure how much detail to have in the booklet, or even if we should use a booklet. You might have some ideas on that. We discovered one or two glitches we're glad we found before throwing it open to unsuspecting others. The music will vary. You'll recognise this one! Sometimes we'll use a YouTube video, sometimes perhaps a Taizé chant – mixing it up a little. We've taken bits and pieces from everywhere, and some of Dave Tomlinson's Holy Shed format as well. Hope he doesn't mind! Would welcome your comments. Will let you know the date of the first gathering. This is so exciting!

To which I emailed back:

"Happy to help, Hope. Happy to help. Sounds fantastic. Any new groups which could almost be called 'church' need to be started by your generation, not mine."

Welcome

to

Shalom Space

Shalom Space is an intentional spiritual gathering
where all are welcome,
whatever you believe or whatever you do not believe

Our commitment to each other

All conversation and comments made here are held in trust.
'What's said in the room stays in the room.'
You are not expected to believe
what you said you believed the last time we met.
We speak only for ourselves,
listening respectfully to others without interruption.

Today's theme is
'Compassion and Inclusion'

Arriving

We invite you to take a stone from the bucket.

During the time for coffee and greetings think about what the theme suggests to you.

Greeting Each Other

The coffee etc. is free, though a koha is appreciated

Gathering

Please sit in the circle of chairs and join in the Gathering statement responsively.

> In this place all are welcome
> **The tall, the thin, the shy and the 'out there'**
> In this place all are accepted
> **Cis and trans, gay lesbian, straight, bisexual and non-binary**
> In this place all are loved
> **Simply because we are all human beings.**
> **In this place all are honoured.**

Lighting of the Candle

The candle represents the light of the spirit which is always among us.

Stories of the Stones

We invite you to 'check in' one-by-one, using your time to talk about your week or about how the theme resonates with you. Place your stones around the candle on the floor at the centre of the group where the unlit tea light candles are laid out.

Candle Community

As we light the candles, we remember people we love and those who especially need our support at this time.

Readings

Matthew 14:14

When Jesus went ashore he saw a great crowd,
and he had compassion on them and healed their sick.

Karen Armstrong: The Charter of Compassion

"The principle of compassion lies at the heart of all religious, ethical and spiritual traditions, calling us always to treat all others as we wish to be treated ourselves. Compassion impels us to work tirelessly to alleviate the suffering of our fellow creatures, to dethrone ourselves from the centre of our world and put another there, and to honour the inviolable sanctity of every single human being, treating everybody, without exception, with absolute justice, equity and respect.

It is also necessary in both public and private life to refrain consistently and empathically from inflicting pain. To act or speak violently out of spite, chauvinism, or self-interest, to impoverish, exploit or deny basic rights to anybody, and to incite hatred by denigrating others – even our enemies – is a denial of our common humanity.…

We urgently need to make compassion a clear, luminous and dynamic force in our polarized world. Rooted in a principled determination to transcend selfishness, compassion can break down political, dogmatic, ideological and religious boundaries. Born of our deep interdependence, compassion is essential to human relationships and to a fulfilled humanity. It is the path to enlightenment, and indispensable to the creation of a just economy and a peaceful global community."[74]

Reflection/Input

Affirmation

Said together. Join in where you can.

A caring community,
where everyone is valued and included regardless,
takes time and effort.

It requires paying attention
to those who may get lost among the crowd;

It requires compassion
for those who struggle;
It requires grace
for making space for those who are different;

It depends upon
a lack of possessiveness or territoriality;
It depends upon
dissolution of 'us' and 'them' thinking;
It depends upon
a firm centre with a permeable boundary
so anyone can enter and find their place
in relation to that centre
which holds us all together.

We here today affirm our intention
to give that time,
apply that effort
and seek that grace
so all truly feel welcome here.

Free For All

Time to respond, ask questions, agree, disagree, respectfully communicate as you wish.

Toast To Life

A toast to life in gratitude for all we have been given.

We are given many gifts,
among them the created world of this planet,
hanging like a blue teardrop in the inky blackness of space.

Today we toast this life as grateful beings,
ready to do our part to save this planet
so its waters may always be blue and pure,
its forests green and lush and its creatures safe and 'here.'
To life!
To life!

Music to Reflect on

'Let us reach down deep inside us'
A hymn about finding the Self within

Let us reach down deep inside us
to the place where quiet reigns;
Find the Self who lives inside us
knows our joy and knows our pains:
Let our ego stand aside there,
shadow sharing space with light.
Let our inner selves rejoice at how
Love shines in darkest night.

Wind and fire and earthquake pass
but Spirit is not found in them;
Still, small voice is hardly heard,
but brings Love which does not condemn.
In lives buffeted by windstorms,
rocked by quakes and scorched by fire,
stillness brings surprising solace
as we find there, hearts' desire.

Sacred calm means minds can settle,
hearts grow quiet, souls grow still;
Busy thinking slows its rhythm,
gives compassion chance to fill.
Even long-forgotten scars heal
as new balm brings a new way;
Every space and every crevice
warms as Love arrives to stay.[75]

Words © 2015 Susan Jones
Tune Gaelic Traditional Melody. Arr © John Bell.
Faith Forever Singing 10(i)

Blessing (Said together)

For those who look for love, but are abused,
For those who have lost family and friends,

For those who live where there is strife or war,
We have lit the candle of compassion.

As we leave this space of Shalom,
We seek to act compassionately
towards all whom we encounter on the journey of life.

Silence

We invite you to walk the labyrinth in the inner courtyard of SHALOM, stay inside for more coffee and chat, or move between the two spaces.

Thank you for coming. We hope you will want to return.

If you wish, leave us your email so we can let you know of future events.

Hope and Charlie,
Travellers on the Way.

Endnotes

1 'Good' included the usual keeping of the commandments, honesty, integrity but also a fairly draconian position on no pre-marital sex.

2 Jean Piaget (1896-1980) was a Swiss psychologist interested in child development. He developed a stage theory describing developmental milestones.

3 James Fowler III (1940-2015) was an American theologian. He was Professor of Theology and Human Development at Emory University. He published a developmental stage theory of faith in 1981.

4 Morgan Scott Peck (1936-2005) was an American psychiatrist and best-selling author who wrote the book *The Road Less Traveled*, in 1978. His stages of faith were included in his 1987 book *The Different Drum. Community Making and Peace.*

5 Marcus Joel Borg (1942-2015) was an American New Testament scholar and theologian. He was a fellow of the Jesus Seminar and a major figure in historical Jesus scholarship.

6 Thomas Moore (b. 1940) is a Jungian psychotherapist, former monk, and writer. His book *Care of the Soul* was published in 1992. He writes and lectures in the fields of archetypal psychology, mythology, and imagination. His work is influenced by the writings of Carl Jung and James Hillman.

7 Some fairy tales are not light pieces of childish nonsense. See Clarissa Pinkola Estés' work.

8 PK is a shortened nickname for Preacher's kid – the child of a clergy person.

9 Ranier Maria Rilke, *Letters to a Young Poet* (Leipzig: Insel Verlag, 1929). "Be patient toward all that is unsolved in your heart and try to love the questions themselves, like locked rooms and like books that are now written in a very foreign tongue. Do not now seek the answers, which cannot be given you because you would not be able to live them. And the point is, to live everything. Live the questions now. Perhaps you will then gradually, without noticing it, live along some distant day into the answer." https://www.columbia.edu/~ey2172/rilke.html Accessed 24 September 2021.

10 Marcus Borg, *Convictions: How I Learned What Matters Most* (Harper One, 2014).

11 Edward Farley, *Theologia: The Fragmentation and Unity of Theological Education* (Fortress Press, 1983).

12 https://en.wikipedia.org/wiki/Industrial_Revolution Accessed 24 September 2021.

13 John Dominic Crossan, *Who is Jesus?* (Westminster John Knox Press, 1996), p. 79.

14 David Tacey, *Religion As Metaphor: Beyond Literal Belief* (Transaction Publishers, 2015), p. xiii.

15 ibid.

16 *Hollow Man*, 2000.

17 Also, in staying on your own island and not venturing to visit others, you might never learn of the different ways other islands celebrated the ocean which was common to them all.

18 Edward Edinger *Ego and Archetype: Individuation and the Religious Function of the Psyche* (Shambala, reissue edition 2017).

19 Martin Buber's *I and Thou* was originally published in German in 1937.

20 Matthew Martin and Eric W. Cowan, 'Remembering Martin Buber and the I–Thou in counselling,' *Counseling Today: A Publication of the American Counseling Association*, 8 May 2019, https://ct.counseling.org/2019/05/remembering-martin-buber-and-the-i-thou-in-counseling/ Accessed 24 September 2021.

21 ibid.

22 https://edgestudio.com/script/sams-speech-worth-fighting-for/ Accessed 24 September 2021.

23 https://www.goodreads.com/quotes/305556-sam-i-wonder-if-we-ll-ever-be-put-into-songs Accessed 24 September 2021.

24 'On Death' from *The Prophet*, https://poets.org/poem/death Accessed 23 October 2021.

25 Dave Tomlinson's *The Holy Shed* YouTube videos, especially week 40, mention this concept of day and night language.

26 Online article covering an interview with Bishop John Spong. 'An interview with John Shelby Spong: "I am very orthodox after all!"' by Scott Stephens. Posted by Ben Myers. 5 September 2007. https://www.faith-theology.com/2007/09/interview-with-john-shelby-spong-i-am.html Accessed 24 September 2021.

27 Sue Monk Kidd, *When the Heart Waits: Spiritual Direction for Life's Sacred Questions* (HarperCollins, 1990); *The Dance of the Dissident Daughter: A Woman's Journey from Christian Tradition to the Sacred Feminine* (HarperOne, 1996).

28 Brian McLaren, *A New Kind of Christian: A Tale of Two Friends on a Spiritual Journey* (Jossey-Bass, January 2001); *The Story We Find Ourselves In: Further Adventures of a New Kind of Christian* (Jossey-Bass, February 2003); *The Last Word and the Word After That: A Tale of Faith, Doubt, and a New Kind of Christianity* (Jossey-Bass, April 2005).

29 Brian McLaren, *Generous Orthodoxy: Why I Am a Missional, Evangelical, Post/Protestant, Liberal/Conservative, Mystical/Poetic, Biblical, Charismatic/ Contemplative, Fundamentalist/Calvinist, Anabaptist/Anglican, Methodist, Catholic, Green, Incarnational, Depressed-yet-Hopeful, Emergent, Unfinished CHRISTIAN* (Zondervan, 2004); *A New Kind of Christianity* (HarperOne, 2010); *Why Did Jesus, Moses, the Buddha, and Mohammed Cross the Road? Christian Identity in a Multi-Faith World* (Jericho Books, 2012); *Faith After Doubt: Why Your Beliefs Stopped Working and What to Do About It* (St. Martin's Press, 2021).

30 Brian McLaren, *Finding Our Way Again: The Return of the Ancient Practices* (Thomas Nelson, 2008); *Naked Spirituality: A Life With God in 12 Simple Words* (HarperOne, 2011); *We Make the Road by Walking: A Year-Long Quest for Spiritual Formation, Reorientation, and Activation* (Jericho Books, 2014); *Seeking Aliveness: Daily Reflections on a New Way to Experience and Practise the Christian Faith* (Hodder & Stoughton, 2017).

31 Karen Armstrong, *Through the Narrow Gate* (Pan Books, 1982).

32 Karen Armstrong, *A History of God* (Ballantine Books, 1993); *The Spiral Staircase: My Climb Out Of Darkness* (Knopf Publishing, 2004); *A Short History of Myth* (Canongate, 2005); *The Bible: A Biography* (Atlantic Monthly Press, 2007); *The Case for God.* (Vintage, 2009); *Twelve Steps to a Compassionate Life* (Vintage, 2011).

33 Barbara Brown Taylor, *Home By Another Way* (Cowley Publications, 1999); *Speaking of Sin: The Lost Language of Salvation* (Cowley Publications, 2001); *Leaving Church: A Memoir of Faith* (HarperOne, 2007); *An Altar in the World: A Geography of Faith* (HarperOne, 2009); *Learning to Walk in the Dark* (HarperOne, 2014); *Holy Envy: Finding God in the Faith of Others* (HarperOne, 2019).

34 Dave Tomlinson, *The Post-Evangelical* (Zondervan, 2003); *I Shall Not Want* (SPCK, 2006); *Re-enchanting Christianity* (Canterbury Press, 2008); *How to be a bad Christian – and a better human being* (Hodder & Stoughton, 2012); *The Bad Christian's Manifesto* (Hodder & Stoughton, 2014).

35 Rob Bell, *Velvet Elvis: Repainting the Christian Faith* (Zondervan, 2005); *Everything is Spiritual* (DVD) (Zondervan, 2007); *The Gods Aren't Angry* (DVD) (Flannel, 2008); *Jesus Wants to Save Christians: A Manifesto for the Church in Exile* (Zondervan, 2008); *Drops Like Stars: A Few Thoughts on Creativity and Suffering* (Zondervan, 2009); *Love Wins* (Harper One, 2011);

What We Talk About When We Talk About God (HarperOne 2013); *How to be Here* (Harper Collins 2016); *NOOMA Videos; What Is the Bible?* (HarperOne 2017).

36 For example, Edinger's books which deal with a Jungian approach to scripture. Edward Edinger, *Ego and Archetype: Individuation and the Religious Function of the Psyche* (Shambhala, reissue edition 2017); *Encounter With the Self: A Jungian Commentary on William Blake's Illustrations of the Book of Job* (Inner City Books, 1986); *The Bible and the Psyche: Individuation Symbolism in the Old Testament* (Inner City Books, 1986); *The Christian Archetype: A Jungian Commentary on the Life of Christ* (Inner City Books 1987); *Transformation of the God-Image: An Elucidation of Jung's Answer to Job* (Inner City Books 1992); *Ego and Self: The Old Testament Prophets From Isaiah to Malachi* (Inner City Books 2000); *The Sacred Psyche: A Psychological Approach to the Psalms* (Inner City Books 2003).

37 Cynthia Bourgeault, *Wisdom Way of Knowing: Reclaiming an Ancient Tradition to Awaken the Heart* (Jossey-Bass, 2003); *Centering prayer and inner awakening.* Foreword by Thomas Keating (Cowley Publications, 2004); *Chanting the Psalms* (New Seeds, 2006); *The Wisdom Jesus: Transforming Heart and Mind – A New Perspective on Christ and His Message* (Shambhala, 2008); *The Meaning of Mary Magdalene: Discovering the Woman at the Heart of Christianity* (Shambhala, 2010); *The Holy Trinity and the Law of Three: Discovering the Radical truth at the Heart of Christianity* (Shambhala, 2013); *The Heart of Centering Prayer: Nondual Christianity in Theory and Practice* (Shambhala, 2016); *Eye of the Heart: a Spiritual Journey into the Imaginal Realm* (Shambhala, 2020).

38 John 15:13.

39 ibid.

40 Interview with Bishop John Spong, ibid.

41 David Griebner, *The Carpenter and the Unbuilder* (Upper Room, 1996).

42 Caroline Myss From *The Power of Holy Language* podcast of Tami Simons with Caroline Myss https://resources.soundstrue.com/podcast/caroline-myss-the-power-of-holy-language/ Accessed 24 September 2021.

43 Written by Dinah Mulock Craik, a 19th century novelist in *A Life for a Life*. (Facsimilie reprint – Kessinger Publishing, 2004).

44 David Gushee, *Changing Our Mind: A call from America's leading evangelical ethics scholar for full acceptance of LGBT Christians in the Church.* (Read The Spirit Books, 2014).

45 David Gushee, *Still Christian: Following Jesus Out of American Evangelism* (Westminster John Knox Press, 2017); *After Evangelicalism: The Path to a New Christianity* (Westminster John Knox Press, 2020).

46 Brian McLaren, "Foreword" in David P Gushee, *After Evangelicalism: The Path to a New Christianity*, (Westminster John Knox Press, 2020, p. xi.).

47 Ezekiel 37:25.

48 Romans 6:4.

49 English Separatists separated themselves from English Anglicanism and were known as dissenters. Several different dissenting groups formed during the commonwealth period when the English monarchy was disrupted.

50 This story ends in Genesis 45.

51 Passover also has other symbols, e.g. bitter herbs.

52 The crucifixion account goes to some length to explain that Jesus' body wasn't broken, as he was already dead when the soldiers checked his body. Breaking the legs of the dying person meant they could not stand up on their feet and draw in a breath, so they died more quickly.

53 At the time, the Moro chocolate bar was being advertised as "Get more go on Moro" and the advertising for Red Bull energy drinks promised they would "give you wings." (Other chocolate bars and energy drinks are available!).

54 Phyllis Tickle, *The Great Emergence: How Christianity Is Changing and Why* (Baker Books, 2008).

55 David Tacey, *The Spirituality Revolution* (HarperCollins, 2003).

56 David Tacey, *Beyond Literal Belief: Religion as Metaphor* (Garratt Publishing, 2015) & (Routledge, 2015). Note that the title and sub-title are swapped in some editions.

57 David Tacey, *The Darkening Spirit: Jung, Spirituality, Religion* (Routledge, 2013).

58 https://www.politico.com/news/2021/01/20/joe-biden-sworn-in-as-president-inaugural-address-460750. Accessed 24 September 2021.

59 David Tacey, *How to read Jung* (Granta Publications, 2015) in Chapter 10. https://books.google.co.nz/books/about/How_to_Read_Jung.html?id=y3YQAQAAIAAJ&redir_esc=y Accessed 24 September 2021.

60 ibid.

61 David M. Odorisio 'The Sacred Psyche' https://www.ahomeforsoul.com/sacred-psyche Accessed 24 September 2021.

62 Mary Oliver Tarset, *Wild Geese* (Bloodaxe, 2004).

63 'Nativity' by Joy Cowley included in "*Spirit in a Strange Land: a selection of New Zealand spiritual verse*," edited by Paul Morris, Harry Ricketts & Mike Grimshaw (Random House, 2002).

64 Carol Ann Duffy 'Prayer' *The Times Saturday Review*, 1992. The last four names are islands off the British Coast. The prayer on the radio to which Duffy refers is the shipping weather forecast.

65 Dave Tomlinson, *Black Sheep and Prodigals: An antidote to black and white religion* (Hodder & Stoughton, 2017) p. 59.

66 Dave Tomlinson posted a weekly reflection from *The Holy Shed* from the beginning of the global pandemic of 2020/2021 https://www.youtube.com/watch?v=Oz1W7MKeGeo&t=110s Accessed 24 September 2021.

67 https://stethelburgas.org/event/monthly-soul-space/ Accessed 24 September 2021.

68 https://www.sundayassembly.com/board-of-trustees/ Accessed 24 September 2021.

69 https://www.sundayassembly.com/our-mission/ Accessed 24 September 2021.

70 http://sunday.org.nz/about/ Accessed 24 September 2021.

71 http://sunday.org.nz/about/ Accessed 24 September 2021.

72 London Sunday Assembly website, ibid.

73 ibid.

74 https://charterforcompassion.org/charter Accessed 24 September 2021.

75 This hymn will be included in *Progressing on the Journey: Lyrics and liturgy for a conscious church* by Susan Jones, to be published by Philip Garside Publishing Ltd.

Copyright

Email Susan at: jones.rs@xtra.co.nz

Special thanks to Trish Patrick for
her help with the author description

Paperback International 2021:
ISBN 9781988572864

Also available

Paperback print-on-demand USA: ISBN 9798768125127
New Zealand paperback edition: ISBN 9781988572826
ePub: ISBN 9781988572833
Kindle/Mobi: ISBN 9781988572840
PDF edition: ISBN 9781988572857

Philip Garside Publishing Ltd
PO Box 17160
Wellington 6147
New Zealand

books@pgpl.co.nz — www.pgpl.co.nz

Cover photograph of wetlands boardwalk
at Pauahatanui Inlet, Porirua
by Alexander Garside — Garside Imaging

Coffee cups line art
by Rosemary Garside

Forthcoming books by Susan Jones to be published by Philip Garside Publishing Ltd

We are All Equally Human:
Conversations in a Coffee Shop Book 2

Charity, a young lesbian church goer, attends her church's national conference, and finds herself hurt and upset by the swirl of the 'gay debate' in the Church. She comes home puzzled and worried.

Charity and her minister plunge into coffee shop conversations about this issue.

Being Woman in the World:
Conversations in a Coffee Shop Book 3

Faith's weekly coffee bar conversations with her minister explore the Feminine – in psychology and theology, women in biblical texts, roles in church and society, God and gender, women and spirituality. They cover the range!

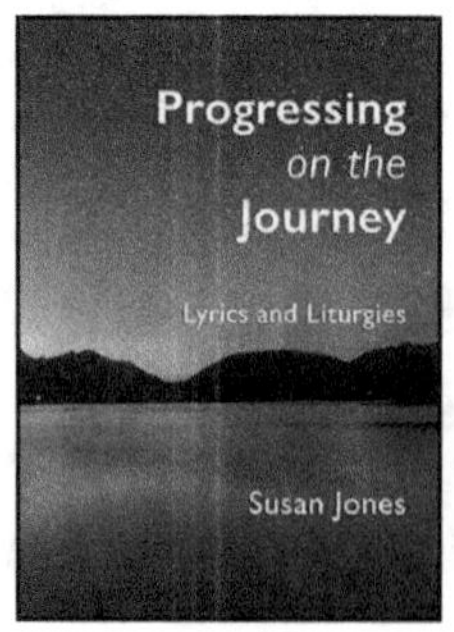

Progressing on the Journey:
Lyrics and liturgy for a conscious church

Music for 40 new hymns, set to well known tunes, which address contemporary issues and celebrate the church year.

This book also contains a wealth of responsive prayers and liturgy for worship.

Includes: Gatherings, Creeds, Affirmations, Communion liturgies, Blessings, poems and two Reflections.

www.ingramcontent.com/pod-product-compliance
Lightning Source LLC
Chambersburg PA
CBHW071944190726
48293CB00004B/1338